Praise for the novels of M. Leighton

DOWN TO YOU

"OMG! It was freakin' hot! . . . M. Leighton knows how to make sexy bad boys that can steal your breath with a single look. *Down to You* will have you hooked after page one! It was a fantastic book!"
—*Nette's Bookshelf*

"Did me in from [the] very first strip club scene. Done . . . stick a fork in me! I mean, bad boy being, motorcycle riding, tattoo having, emotional baggage carrying, tall dark and sexy looking, smart as a whip but hiding it—you know what that does to me. Seriously, what . . . is it with the bad boy that makes me lose my mind? I know I'm not alone here."
—*Scandalicious Book Reviews*

"Steamy, sexy, and super hot! M. Leighton completely and absolutely knocked [it] out of the park."
—*The Bookish Brunette*

"M. Leighton is quickly becoming one of my favorite contemporary romance writers. *Down to You* is scorching hot . . . an emotional roller coaster. I recommend *Down to You* to all contemporary romance readers out there for sure."
—*Reading Angel*

"From its sexy, awesome opening sequence to the jaw-dropping end, *Down to You* is a story that will keep you laughing and swooning . . . Surprising, sexy, and fun, *Down to You* is a book that will steam you up and have you guessing until the very last page."
—*The Bookish Babe*

"A funny, sexy, suspenseful read."
—*Romance Lovers Book Blog*

"I loved *Down to You*. I devoured it, and I'm pretty sure you will, too."
—*For Love and Books*

"Takes readers on a wild ride filled with twists and turns and moments that'll leave you ready for a cold shower! [Leighton's] story has it all and then some."
—*A Life Bound by Books*

continued . . .

UP TO ME

"Scorching hot . . . insanely intense . . . and it is shocking. *Shocking!*"
—*The Bookish Babe*

"I definitely did NOT see the twists coming."
—*The Book List Reviews*

"You know those first books in a series that totally blow you away and you just think, wow, this just can't get any better than this? I mean, how can you make perfection better after all? Well, no worries here. Not only did [Leighton] completely blow *Down to You* out of the water with *Up to Me*, but she took it even further."
—*My Guilty Obsession*

"Brilliant . . . Cash is seriously one of my most favorite characters ever. He's a true alpha male, and you know how much I love those! He's just one sexy beast."
—*The Book Goddess*

"Leighton never gives the reader a chance to catch her breath . . . The plot has so many unexpected twists and turns that my heart was racing along . . . fast-paced, edge of your seat thrills. Yes, there is sex, OMG tongue hanging out of mouth, scorching sex."
—*Literati Literature Lovers*

"Well, I drank this one down in one huge gulp . . . and it was delicious. How . . . hot is Cash? Oh my god, and the sex. The sex in this book is seriously *scandalicious*."
—*Scandalicious Book Reviews*

"With twists happening faster than you can turn the page, Leighton continues her epic action and romance with characters that just keep getting hotter and hotter."
—*A Life Bound by Books*

"Delicious . . . I stopped reading in order to grab a cold beer and cool off . . . the twists and turns on the plot line are brilliant."
—*Review Enthusiast*

DOWN TO YOU

The Bad Boys, Book 1

M. LEIGHTON

BERKLEY BOOKS, NEW YORK

THE BERKLEY PUBLISHING GROUP
Published by the Penguin Group
Penguin Group (USA) Inc.
375 Hudson Street, New York, New York 10014, USA

USA I Canada I UK I Ireland I Australia I New Zealand I India I South Africa I China

Penguin Books Ltd., Registered Offices: 80 Strand, London WC2R 0RL, England
For more information about the Penguin Group, visit penguin.com.

Library of Congress Cataloging-in-Publication Data

Leighton, M.
Down to you / M. Leighton. —Berkley trade paperback edition.
pages cm—(The Bad Boys ; Book 1)
ISBN 978-0-425-26984-8 (alk. paper)
1. Triangles (Interpersonal relations)—Fiction.   2. Erotic fiction.   I. Title.
PS3612.E3588D69   2013
813'.6—dc23   2013007805

PUBLISHING HISTORY
Smashwords edition / 2012
Berkley trade paperback edition / July 2013

PRINTED IN THE UNITED STATES OF AMERICA

10 9 8 7 6 5 4 3 2 1

Cover art by Thinkstock
Cover design by Lesley Worrell

To my husband

You've loved and supported me through this entire crazy journey, and you've celebrated the most amazing times of my life with me. Thank you for hanging around. I'm glad you decided to keep me.

To Courtney Cole

My crit partner and one of the best friends a girl could ask for. I love you, chica, and I want you to move next door. Get right on that. Thanks.

To the Indie Hellcats

Without your late-night input, this project wouldn't have its gorgeous face. Your love and support is unfailing, amazing, and humbling. I am forever grateful to Georgia Cates for bringing me into your midst.

I love you all.

And, as always, most of all **to my God**.

You're everything. That is all.

ONE

Olivia

My head is spinning lightly, but happily. I can't even remember the name of the drinks Shawna keeps ordering for us. I just know they're delicious. And potent as hell! Wow!

"When's the stripper coming? I'm ready to get my freak on!" Ginger shouts. She's the crazy, outspoken, cougar-of-a-bartender we work with at Tad's Sports Bar and Grill in Salt Springs, Georgia. She's wild enough in her natural environment, but stick her in a strange new place in a city like Atlanta and she morphs into a full-blown tiger. *Rawr!*

She looks at me and grins. Her bottle-blond hair looks urine-yellow in the low light and her pale blue eyes are twinkling devilishly.

I'm instantly suspicious.

"What?" I ask dazedly.

"I talked to the manager ahead of time. He's gonna make sure Shawna has to help the stripper get out of those pesky clothes he'll be wearing." She giggles maniacally. I can't help but laugh. She's a mess.

"Ryan would kill her if she stripped another man's clothes off, bachelorette party or not!"

"He'll never know. What stays in the VIP room happens in the VIP room," she slurs.

"Don't you mean what *happens* in the VIP room *stays* in the VIP room?"

"That's what I said."

I snicker. "Oh, okay."

I giggle as I watch her take another sip of her neurotoxic drink. I opt for my water instead. Somebody has to remain semilucid. Might as well be me. Tonight is all about Shawna, anyway. I want to send her off into married life with the best party possible. I doubt that includes her having to carry me home or clean my vomit off her shoes.

A knock at the door to the private room has us all turning our heads in that direction. The girls immediately start laughing and hollering and catcalling.

Dear God, I hope it's the stripper and not a cop or something!

The door opens and in walks the most incredibly handsome guy I think I've ever seen. He looks like he's in his early twenties, really tall, and built like a football player—wide chest and shoulders, thick arms and legs, tiny waist in between. He's dressed in solid black from head to toe. But it's his face that's most impressive.

Sweet hell, he's effin' gorgeous!

His short hair is dark blond and his face is chiseled perfection. I can't tell what color his eyes are as he scans the room, but I can see that they're dark. He's just opened his mouth to speak when his gaze finally makes its way to me. His eyes click to a stop on mine and he stares.

I'm completely mesmerized. As I look into them, I still can't determine a color, but the orbs look nearly black. Even in the light spilling through the door behind him, they look like pools of ink. Just barely, he cocks his head to the side as he watches me.

It makes me nervous. And excited. I don't know why. I have no reason to be nervous *or* excited. But I am. He makes me feel twitchy. Squirmy. Warm.

We're still staring at each other when Ginger gets up and drags him farther into the room, flinging the door shut behind him.

"All right, Shawna. Come kick your single life to the curb the right way!"

The other girls start squealing and cheering her on. Shawna's smiling but shaking her head. "No way! Not this girl!" The bridesmaids-to-be get more insistent, two of them coming around to take her by the hands and haul her to her feet.

She leans back, away from them, shaking her head more vigorously. "No, no, no. I don't want to. One of y'all do it."

She starts wiggling her arms to free herself, but the girls have a death grip on her thin wrists. When she looks at me, her wide brown eyes tell me all I need to know. She's totally freaked by the idea.

"Liv, help!" I raise my hands in a gesture that says, *What do you want me to do?* She nods toward the hunk hulking behind Ginger. "You do it!"

"Are you crazy? I'm not stripping a stripper!"

"Please! You know I'd do it for you."

And she would. Dammit.

How the hell does the world's clumsiest shy girl get wrangled into doing things like this?

As I so often do, I answer myself.

Because she's a pushover!

Taking a deep breath, I stand and turn toward Hot Stripper Guy, purposely jacking my chin up another notch. He's still watching me with those smoky coal eyes.

When I take a step toward him, he very slowly raises one eyebrow.

Heat washes through me.

Must be those dangerous drinks, I think. *It has to be.*

I feel flushed and a little breathless, but I take another step, anyway.

Hot Stripper Guy backs away from Ginger and turns to face me fully. He crosses his arms over his chest and waits, that one brow still raised in curiosity. He's not going to make it easy. He's leaving it all up to me, just like Ginger asked them to do.

As if on cue, the music that's been pumping into the room all night gets louder. It's a sexy song, heavy on the bass. It's mood music for sure. It seems to punctuate every intense beat of my heart as I get closer and closer to those velvety eyes.

When I stop in front of him, I have to look up. My five and

a half feet of height is nearly a foot shorter than his towering frame.

Up close, I see that his eyes are brown. Dark, dark brown. Nearly black.

Sinful.

I'm lost in wondering why that particular word would come to mind when the girls start chanting for me to take his shirt off. Uncertainly, I glance at their excited faces, then back to him. Slowly, he spreads his arms, holding them out to his sides, away from his body.

One corner of his mouth twitches. His expression, his body language is rife with challenge.

I realize he doesn't think I'll do it. No one probably does.

And that's exactly why I will.

Letting the beat of the music relax my tense muscles, I plaster a smile on my face as I reach forward to tug Hot Stripper Guy's shirt from the waistband of his pants.

TWO

Cash

Damn, she's beautiful!

Between this girl's black hair, her bright, probably green eyes, her banging little body, and the way she seems a tiny bit shy, I'm wishing we were alone in this room together.

Her smile doesn't leave her lips as she runs her hands around my waist, untucking my shirt. When it's free, she starts to pull it up.

But then she pauses. For a split second, I see her hesitate. She's trying not to show that she's unsure of herself, of what she's doing.

I stare down into those liquid eyes. I don't want her to stop. I want to feel her hands on my skin. So I taunt her, hoping to feed the feline that I'd be willing to bet is buried somewhere down deep.

"Oh, come on. Is that all you got?" I whisper.

Her eyes bore into mine and I hold my breath, waiting to see which side will win. In fascination, I watch as the balance of power shifts and the change is reflected in her eyes. They get a little brighter, a little feistier. I've never actually *seen* someone muster courage. Determination. Something in this girl refuses to give in, to back down. She's rising to the challenge. And it's hot as hell.

She keeps her eyes on mine as she starts to pull up my shirt. She leans in closer and I get a whiff of her perfume. It's sweet and a little musky. Sexy. Just like her.

She has to plaster her body to mine and stretch up on her tiptoes to get my shirt over my head. I can feel her breasts pushing against my chest. I could make the task easier for her. But I don't. I like the feel of her rubbing against me. There's no way I'm ruining that.

Once she has my shirt off, she backs up and looks me over. She's shy about it. That much is obvious. It's like she wants to look, but she's a little embarrassed to, which actually makes it more of a turn-on for some reason. I'm sure every other eye in the room is watching me, watching *us*, but hers are the only ones I can feel. They're like tongues of fire, licking my skin. They're searing and tangible. Or at least they feel that way to me.

I take a deep breath and her eyes drop to my stomach. Then they flicker down a little farther. She stares longer than she should but not nearly as long as I want her to.

I start to get hard.

Her eyes widen and her lips fall open just enough for her tongue to sneak out and wet them. I have to grit my teeth to keep from pulling her to me and kissing that lush little mouth of hers.

Then light pours into the room. It's just enough to break the spell.

I hear a man's voice. A very pissed-off man's voice.

"Dude, what the hell?" It's Jason. I know why he's angry.

It's not easy to tear my eyes away from hers. There's a shy, reluctant excitement in them that makes me want to see how far I can push her. But I don't. Push her, that is. Instead, I look away, turning my head to glance first at Jason and then at the room of salivating females. The jig is up.

Damn. That was shaping up to be quite a diversion.

I smile into the group of faces riveted on me. "Ladies, this is Jason. He'll be entertaining you tonight."

All eyes turn to Jason as he closes the door and moves around me. I look at the girl that's holding my shirt. She's perplexed. And for good reason.

"What do you mean, he'll be entertaining us?" she asks, turning her confused eyes on me.

I don't answer her right away. I know she'll figure it out soon enough.

She looks over at Jason, trying to piece together what just happened.

"Now, which one of you beautiful women is the bride-to-be?" Jason asks.

I see it the instant understanding dawns. Her eyes widen again, and even in the low light, I see her cheeks turn red.

She looks back to me and frowns.

"If he's the stripper, then who are you?"

"I'm Cash Davenport. I own the club."

THREE

Olivia

I can't help but stare, openmouthed, at the owner. I fight the urge to look for a table to crawl under. I've never been more mortified in all my life.

I hear the girls clucking over Jason, but it barely penetrates my mind, my focus. Every other piece of gray matter is concentrated squarely on the guy standing in front of me.

And then I get angry.

"Why did you let me do that? Why didn't you say something or introduce yourself?"

He smiles. *Smiles*, dammit! It registers for a second that it's a stunning smile, but then my humiliation returns and overshadows it completely.

"Why would I do that, when letting you undress me was so much more fun?"

"Um, because it's completely unprofessional, for one thing."

"How is that? You ladies ordered a stripper. Does it matter who I send?"

"That's not the point. You were being purposely deceptive."

He chuckles. *Chuckles*, dammit! The nerve. "I don't remember agreeing to send you an *honest* stripper. Just a willing one."

I clamp my lips shut. He's infuriating.

Nonchalantly, as though he's not standing in front of me with no shirt on, he crosses his arms over his chest. The action draws my attention to his perfectly rounded pecs and the tattoo that covers one whole side. I can't make out exactly what it is, but part of it even reaches out and spreads over his left shoulder, like long, jagged fingers.

He clears his throat and my eyes fly to his face. He's smiling even wider now and I feel my scowl roll into place. I can't think straight with him standing here like this. He's far too disconcerting with his shirt off.

"Don't you think you should at least get dressed?"

"Don't you think you should at least give me my shirt, then?"

I look down and sure enough, clutched tightly in my fisted hand, is his black T-shirt. Angrily, I toss it at him. And he catches it.

Dammit!

The strange thing is, even as I seethe, I'm not sure why I'm so mad. I just know that I am.

"You sure are full of fire! Maybe I should've taken *your* shirt off instead," he says as he pulls his tee over his head.

"What difference would that have made?"

Other than it would have been about ten times more *embarrassing.*

He stops and grins at me, a cocky sexy grin that I don't want to be affected by, but I can't seem to help myself. "If I had, you sure as hell wouldn't be *mad* right now."

My mouth goes bone dry as a mental image of that scene flickers in and out of my mind—him easing my shirt over my head, his hands on my skin, his body pressed to mine, his lips so close I can almost taste them. That's all it takes to make me forget my anger.

I'm staring at him with my mouth open—again—as he tucks his shirt back in. When he's finished, he takes a step closer to me. I stand perfectly still. His grin fades into a seductive curve of his lips that makes my knees feel funny. I'm completely spellbound and embarrassingly turned on when he bends to whisper in my ear.

"You'd better close those lips before I'm tempted to kiss them and *really* give you something to be all hot and bothered about."

I suck in a breath. I'm shocked. But not by his statement. By the fact that I really want him to do exactly that, by the fact that it makes my stomach tighten just thinking about it.

He leans back and looks down at me. I'm not sure why, but I snap my lips shut.

And he notices.

Dammit!

I see disappointment flicker across his face. And, perversely, that pleases me.

"Maybe next time, then," he says with a wink. Clearing his throat, he steps back and looks to his left. "Ladies," he says, nodding to the other girls, girls who are paying him zero attention as they watch Jason tease Shawna with his now-bare upper body. He looks back at me and, in a decidedly Southern way, says, "Ma'am."

He nods once, then turns, opens the door, and walks out, closing it quietly behind him.

Never before have I been so tempted to chase someone.

I crack open my lids a tiny bit, fully expecting to feel knives stabbing me in the head. But the bright, early September light pouring through the window isn't painful at all. It's the strange case of the hangover that never was. And I'm grateful.

What *is* painful, however, is remembering the humiliation of the night before. It comes back to me in a rush, as does the image of the gorgeous club owner, Cash. I roll over and bury my face in the pillow as the details drift through my mind—tall, strong body and perfect, handsome face. A smile to die for.

Ohmigod, he was so effin' hot!

Even now, I wish he'd kissed me. It's ridiculous, but it might've made the whole debacle a little less . . . wasteful.

Chastising myself, I roll onto my back again and stare at the ceiling. I'm smart enough to recognize when I'm giving in to my one true weakness. It's for that reason alone—because of the way my pulse speeds up when I think about his dark eyes daring me to undress him; because of the way I feel all warm when I think about his lips on mine—I have to be glad I'll never see him again. He's the embodiment of the one thing in life I need like a hole in the head—another bad-boy love interest.

As always when I think of disastrous relationships, I think of Gabe. Cash reminds me a lot of him. Cocky, sexy, charming. Untamed. Rebellious.

Heartbreaker.

Gritting my teeth, I drag myself from between the sheets and make my way to the bathroom. I push Gabe out of my head, refuse to give that asshole one more second of my life.

After I've splashed enough cold water on my face to feel partially human, I stumble my way toward the kitchen. I pay little attention to the posh designer furnishings and perfectly placed pieces of art as I pass through the living room. It's been almost two weeks since my roommate bailed and I had to move in with my rich cousin, Marissa. I've finally gotten used to seeing how the other half lives.

Well, sort of, I think as I stop to look at the two-thousand-dollar clock on the wall.

It's nearly eleven. I'm a little irritated with myself for sleeping away a large portion of my day off, so I'm prickly and grumbly when I enter the kitchen. Seeing Marissa sitting on the island with her long, bare legs crossed toward a guy perched on a stool does nothing to help my disposition.

I stare at the back of wide, linen-clad shoulders and a dark blond head. For half a second, I consider what I'm wearing—boy shorts and a tank top—and what I look like: tousled black hair, sleepy green eyes, and smeared mascara. I debate heading straight back to my room, but that option is taken off the table when Marissa speaks to me.

"There you are, Sleeping Beauty!" She smiles warmly in my direction.

I'm immediately wary.

For starters, Marissa is never nice to me. Ever. She is the triple-S trifecta—spoiled, snobby, and snide. If there had been *any* other option for obtaining a roof over my head, I would've chosen it. Not that I'm not grateful. Because I am. And I show that gratitude by paying my share of a rent that Marissa doesn't even pay (her father does) and by *not* strangling her in her sleep. I figure that's pretty generous of me.

"Good morning?" I say uncertainly, my voice hoarse.

The broad shoulders in front of Marissa shift and the dark blond head turns toward me. Sinfully dark brown eyes stop me in my tracks. And steal my breath.

It's Cash. The club owner from last night.

I feel my mouth drop open as my stomach falls through the floor. I'm surprised and embarrassed, but more than anything, I'm overcome by how much more appealing he is in the daylight. In a way, I guess I'd secretly thought my reaction to him last night was a product of alcohol coupled with the fact that I was stripping his clothes off him.

Obviously, neither had anything to do with it.

"What are you doing here?" I ask in confusion.

I see his brow wrinkle. "Pardon me?"

He glances at Marissa, then back to me.

"Wait a minute. Nash, do you know her?" Marissa asks, her warmth now curiously absent.

Nash? Nash, as in Marissa's boyfriend?

I have no idea what to say. My fuzzy mind is having trouble putting puzzle pieces into place.

"Not that I know of," Cash/Nash says, his expression blank.

Once I realize what's going on, my confusion and embarrassment give way to anger and indignation. If there's one thing I hate more than a cheater, it's a liar. Liars disgust and infuriate me.

Reflexively, I rein in my temper. It takes little effort to remain calm now, the result of a lifetime of swallowing my emotions. "Oh, is that right? Do you always so conveniently forget the women who partially undress you?"

Something flashes in his eyes. Is it . . . humor?

"Trust me, I think I'd remember something like that."

Marissa hops off the island and assumes a belligerent stance, her hands fisted on her hips. "What the hell is going on?"

I've never been one to stir up trouble between couples. What they do and don't tell each other is their business. But this time it's different. I don't know why, but it is.

Maybe it's because she's my cousin.

I tell myself that, but I know there's no love lost between Marissa and me. Another thought flies through my head—one that says I'm upset about being so casually forgotten by the guy I woke up thinking about—but I completely disregard it, labeling it ridiculous and moving on.

First, I address Marissa. "Well, *Nash* here showed up at Shawna's bachelorette party last night trying to pass himself off as a club owner named *Cash*." Next, I turn to the imposter in question. Try as I might, I can't keep the derision from my tone. "And you. Really? Cash and Nash? Don't you think you could've been a little more original? What are you, four?"

I fully expect Marissa to throw a holy fit and Cash/Nash to be immediately contrite. Or even to try to lie his way out of what he's done. But what I get is what I least expect.

They both start laughing.

As I look on, confused, it seems only to intensify their amusement. My anger rises accordingly.

It's Cash/Nash who speaks first.

"I guess Marissa didn't happen to mention I have a twin brother, did she?"

FOUR

Nash

I watch the full gamut of emotions play across this girl's beautiful face. Confusion, anger, indignation, pleasure, then confusion again. In the end, her features settle into disbelief.

"You're joking."

"Not hardly. Who would bother to make up a story like that?"

She's still watching me with a dumbfounded look. "So you're Nash."

I nod. "Correct."

"And you have a twin brother named Cash."

"Correct."

"Cash and Nash."

I shrug. "My mother had a thing for country music."

"And Cash owns that club, Dual."

"Correct."

"So, that makes you the lawyer."

"Well, not technically. Not yet, anyway. But, yeah."

"And I'm not being punked."

I laugh. "No, you're not being punked."

She chews the inside of her lip as she digests it all. I don't think she has a clue how sexy and adorable she is.

When it all settles in, she takes a deep breath and asks, "Can I have a do-over?"

I grin. "Sure."

A brilliant smile comes instantly to her lips and she sticks out her hand. "You must be Nash, the boyfriend. I'm Olivia, Marissa's slightly dull cousin."

I grin. "It's nice to meet you, Olivia, Marissa's slightly dull cousin."

I doubt there's one single dull thing about you.

She nods her head in satisfaction and turns to walk to the coffeepot. It's all I can do not to watch her. I have to *make* myself focus on the beautiful blonde in front of me. I've only ever looked at Marissa and seen an elegant, statuesque, gorgeous woman. But this morning, I find myself wishing she were a cute, rumpled, fiery brunette instead.

Shit! That's not good!

FIVE

Olivia

"Ohmigod! You can't be serious!" Shawna mumbles around a mouthful of wedding cake.

I want to laugh at the crumbs flying from between her lips. Coming with her to a cake tasting has been the most fun, second only to heading up the bachelorette party.

"I wish I were joking, but I'm not. It was horrible!" I feel my face flush in remembered embarrassment just from *retelling* what had happened with Nash.

"Well, at least it was the brother and not the one you practically molested."

I slap Shawna's arm. "I *did not* practically molest him!"

"No, but you wanted to."

"I most certainly—"

"Don't even lie to me, you wench! I know you too well. He

had that whole bad-boy thing going on. I'm surprised you didn't wrap your legs and your lips and everything else around him right then and there."

"God, Shawna, you make me sound like some sort of floozy."

"Floozy? Really?" She eyes me skeptically.

We both giggle. Mine turns into full-blown laughter when I see the red icing stuck to Shawna's teeth.

"Shut up. It's a Tracey word," I explain, referring to my mother. She was Miss Prim and Proper. Words like *whore* and *slut* were not even in her vocabulary. Apparently *divorce* and *abandonment* were, though.

"Don't even get me started on her. I will cut a bitch!"

"You know, that's actually kinda scary when you say it now. Your teeth look like you just ate someone's liver." The red food coloring looks like blood in her mouth.

"I did. And it was delicious with a nice Chianti and some fava beans," she says in her best Hannibal Lecter voice, making a strange sucking noise afterward.

We both start laughing, drawing the disapproving eye of the swanky shop's attendant.

"You better shut up. I'm pretty sure it's bad luck to get kicked out of a wedding cake shop a month before your wedding."

Shawna smiles demurely at the attendant, her lips barely moving as she speaks to me. "If you had a piece of coal, we could hold her down, shove it up her ass, and come collect a big fat diamond in a few days."

"I'm pretty sure it takes longer than a few days for coal to turn into a diamond, Shawna."

"Not in that tight ass, it wouldn't."

Casting the stern-faced lady a sidelong glance, I change my mind. "You could be right."

"So, while we've got all this sugary brain food circulating through our blood, let's formulate a plan for you to steal Nash from Marissa. I'm pretty sure it would be the best wedding present *ever* to see the look on that self-righteous whore's face."

"What? Are you crazy? I'm not stealing anyone from anybody!"

"And why not? This guy sounds like everything you've ever wanted."

I sigh. "I know." And Nash does. He's incredibly handsome, charming, obviously intelligent, successful, grounded, responsible—everything my mother had drummed into me since childhood. Everything she thought my father wasn't. And he's not a bad boy, which is the best thing about him. I may not agree with my mother about much, but I know she's right about what kind of guy to set my sights on. I've proven her right time after time after time. Maybe someone like Nash could help the facts get through to my wayward heart. So far, it seems like I'm destined to fall for the wrong guy.

"So then, what's the problem? Go get him."

"It's not that simple. For one thing, I'm not that kind of person."

Shawna drops her fork and looks angrily at me. "And what kind is that, exactly? The kind that goes after what she wants?

The kind that makes life happen for her? The kind that does everything she can to find happiness? Oh, no. You're not that kind at all. You're the martyr. You're the one who's gonna let life pass her by because she won't take risks anymore."

"Wanting to get a degree that I can use to help my father does not make me a martyr."

"No, but giving up on every other area of your life so you can move back to Podunk does."

"He's already had one woman in his life abandon him. I refuse to be the second." I can't keep the sharp edge from my voice. She's stirring up my temper.

"Living your life is not abandonment, Liv."

"That's exactly what *she* said."

To this, Shawna says nothing.

Taking all my core accounting classes up front in my first two years of college was a stroke of genius as far as I'm concerned. But even with a light schedule of easy classes, I'm still tired today for some reason. It's Friday evening and the weekend is just beginning.

And it sucks already.

I'd like to think it's just dread of going home to work all weekend, but I know it's a little more than that. It's that stupid conversation I had with Shawna at the cake tasting.

This guy sounds like everything you've ever wanted.

I sigh. That's becoming clearer with each passing day.

Nash has visited Marissa every single night this week. The

more I hear him talk and see him laugh and observe how he acts, the more I wish I *were* the kind of person who ruthlessly went after what I wanted.

But I'm not. Marissa has the monopoly on that. Well, Marissa and my mother.

If I ever become a thief, Nash will be the first thing I steal.

I can hear his deep voice as he talks to Marissa. No doubt they have exciting plans for the night. Their jet-set lives are the stuff fairy tales are made of. Unfortunately, my life has been anything *but* a fairy tale.

With a resolute jerk that makes my eyes water, I tighten my ponytail. I eye myself in the mirror. Marissa's work uniform is a thousand-dollar suit and Jimmy Choo shoes. Mine is black shorts and a black tee that says *Get a little at Tad's.* A girl like me will never have a life like that.

I'm glad when I hear the front door shut. At least now I don't have to pass the dynamic duo on my way out. It's already a shitty weekend and it's only just begun. Seeing them drool all over each other is the last thing I need.

I give them a couple of minutes' lead before I grab my purse and keys, sling my overnight bag onto my shoulder, and head for the door. I'm thinking to myself that I should've used the bathroom before I left when I look up and see Nash sitting in his sleek black car, talking on the phone. Not watching where I'm going, I forget to step off the curb and end up falling off it instead.

I probably would've been able to keep my balance had I not been loaded down with my stuffed overnight bag. Once it got going in the wrong direction, there was no stopping either of us.

I fall ass over teacup into the parking lot. In my head, I envision myself as a comical cartwheel of flailing arms and legs.

Yep, I'm making a fool of myself. Again. Right in front of Nash.

Is there no end to my embarrassment with this guy?

I'm thinking that as I try to right myself as quickly as possible. Before I can get untangled from my purse and duffel straps, however, strong hands are gripping my arms and hauling me to my feet.

I'm face to face with Nash. His dark-chocolate eyes are full of concern and he smells lightly of expensive cologne, something musky. Dark. Sexy.

"Are you all right?"

I'm discombobulated. "I'm just glad I didn't pee all over myself," I blurt. I see his mouth drop open a tiny bit and I feel my cheeks go up in flames.

Oh sweet Lord, what did I just say?

And then he laughs. His perfect mouth spreads into a wide smile, revealing equally perfect teeth. His face is transformed from gorgeous into just plain breathtaking. And the sound—it's rich and rumbly and slides over my skin like satin.

I know I'm staring, but I can't seem to keep my eyes off the lips that are so close. They look so much like his brother's. So delicious. So forbidden. And, despite all the reasons I shouldn't, I want him to kiss me just as badly.

What the hell is wrong with me?

"I am, too."

My brain is utterly scrambled.

"What?" I ask, dazed and confused.

"I am, too," he repeats.

"You are too what?"

"I'm glad you didn't pee all over yourself, too."

Oh yeah. That.

Apparently, it's the rule of the universe that I make an ass of myself at every possible opportunity with this guy. And his brother, too!

Stepping away from him so I can think, I smile sheepishly and shake my head. "Oh, God! Sorry about that. I, uh, I was just thinking that I should've used the bathroom before I left. I had lots of water today."

I laugh uneasily. He continues to watch me in amusement. It's horrifying.

"Where are you headed?"

"To work."

"Ah. And where's that?" he asks, pushing his hands into his pockets like he's settling in for a long conversation.

"Um, Tad's Bar and Grill in Salt Springs."

"Salt Springs?" He frowns. "That's, what, just over an hour from here?"

"Yep, which is why I need to get going."

I have to get away from him before something more embarrassing happens. Like I reach out and touch the rounded pecs that I can just make out beneath his expensive dress shirt.

"Right. Well, drive carefully."

With a nod and a polite smile, he turns and walks back to the car that's purring quietly a few feet away.

I all but run to my beat-up Honda Civic. It has never looked more welcoming. Or more like an escape pod. I hop in and slam the door, exhaling in relief.

But then, much to my chagrin, I turn the key and hear only a sluggish whine. The engine won't start.

I look at the gas gauge. Half full. It's not an empty tank. I look at the dashboard lights. They're nice and bright. It's not a dead battery. Beyond that, I have no idea what to check.

I'm sitting helplessly behind the wheel, wondering what the hell I'm going to do, when I see Nash cross in front of my car and approach my window. I roll it down.

I try to smile when I feel like crying instead.

"Car won't start?" he asks.

"Nope."

"What seems to be the problem?"

"I have no clue. I have ovaries; therefore, I repel all things mechanical."

He chuckles. "The put-gas-in-it-and-get-the-oil-changed-and-that's-it type, huh?"

"Pretty much."

"Let's take a look. Can you pop the hood?" he asks, rolling his sleeves up to his elbows.

Good Lord, he even has sexy forearms!

I look down and to my left. I see the little symbol for the hood. I'm thankful I at least know where *that* is.

I pull the lever.

I don't know whether I should get out or stay put. For self-preservation purposes, I go with staying put. Remaining in the car, far from Nash, exponentially decreases the likelihood of me doing or saying something stupid. That's always a good thing.

Through the crack where the hood hinges, I can see Nash fiddle with several things, tugging hoses and wires and tightening something down. Then I see him brush his hands off and close the hood.

He walks back to the window. "I don't see anything obviously wrong, but I'm no mechanic. Looks like this car's not going anywhere for a while. Do you want me to call a tow truck?"

I can't help the deep sigh of frustration. "No, that's okay. I can call one after I call in to work."

"Are you sure?"

I muster the brightest smile I can, which isn't very bright at all, I'm sure. "Yeah, I'm sure. Thanks, though."

"Do you want me to wait with you?"

My laugh is bitter. "That's okay. I'd rather get chewed out in private, if you don't mind."

His brow wrinkles. "Are you going to be in trouble?"

I wave my hand dismissively. "Ah, no more than usual."

He nods and starts to walk away but pauses. I see him glance at his watch, then look up. It's obvious the wheels of his mind are turning.

"Why don't you let me drive you to work?"

"Absolutely not! You've got plans with Marissa and it's *way* out of your way. Salt Springs is way out of *everyone's* way."

"We were just going to hang out with some coworkers. I can be a little late. It's not a big deal."

"Well, it is to me. I'll be fine. I appreciate the offer, but I'm gonna have to decline."

"Decline?" he says, his eyes twinkling mischievously. "What if I insist?"

"Insist all you like. My answer won't change."

Nash narrows his eyes at me, and his lips curve up at the corners. He walks slowly to my window and bends down, resting his forearms along the open space. His face is inches from mine.

"I could always make you."

The way he says it sounds dark and dirty and infinitely pleasurable. All I can think of is what I'd like for him to make me do.

There's an unsavory term for that—a guy forcing a girl to do sexual things. But what is it they say? You can't rape the willing. And I'd be willing. Oh, how I'd be willing.

My mouth is so dry, my tongue sticks to the roof. All I can do is shake my head.

Like a flash of lightning, Nash reaches in and snatches the keys from the ignition. His smile is smug when he stands and walks around to the passenger side. He opens the door and collects my overnight bag and my purse from the seat. Before he shuts the door, he says, "It's either come with me or sleep in your car that won't start. Your choice."

With that, he slams the door shut and walks casually away, toting my stuff to his car and dropping it into the backseat. He leans against the driver's door and crosses his arms over his chest to watch me. The challenge is clear.

I'm just stubborn enough that if I *really* didn't want to go with him, I would find a way around him. But therein lies the rub. I *do* want to go with him. Just to spend a little more time with him, without Marissa around, sounds like heaven. I mean, it's not like I have any plans to try to steal him. Or that I even could. Marissa is the total package. She's a whiny bitch, but still, she's gorgeous, wealthy, and successful, and she has hella good connections in the Atlanta world of law.

Then there's me. I'm an accounting-student-slash-bartender-slash-farmer's-daughter. Yeah, stealing Nash isn't an option, even if I were the type to attempt it.

Fortunately, that makes a car ride with him even more harmless.

After rolling up the window, I climb out of the car and lock the door before heading for the plush, cool interior of Nash's BMW. I say nothing about the satisfied smile he's wearing when he slides in beside me. It's better if he thinks he won.

"Now, was that so hard?"

I try to keep my smile slightly on the tolerant side, squashing my exuberance. "I guess not. You drive a hard bargain."

"So I've been told."

"I'm sure you have," I mutter. When Nash's head whips in my direction, I smile innocently. "What?"

He looks suspicious. "I thought you said something."

"Nope. Not me."

I smother my grin as he backs out of the lot.

SIX

Nash

I watch Olivia from the corner of my eye as I steer the car toward the interstate. I know I'm asking for trouble, going to such lengths to spend a little more time with this girl.

It's not that I wouldn't help any female stranded in a similar situation. But would I go this far? Probably not. And would I insist on it? Definitely not.

Why couldn't you just wait with her until a tow truck showed up and then leave?

I don't know the answer to that, but it seems like there's just something about her . . .

She's great looking, no doubt, even though she's not necessarily my type. She's the complete opposite of Marissa in practically every way, physical and otherwise. And, even though

Marissa fits everything in my life to perfection, I don't feel drawn to her like I do this girl.

And that's not good.

And I know it.

Yet here I am. Driving her halfway across the state to drop her off at work. While my girlfriend is waiting for me.

Oh, shit! Marissa!

As I accelerate up the entrance ramp, I turn to Olivia. "Do you mind if I let Marissa know?"

She smiles and shakes her head.

I click a couple of buttons on the console to turn off the Bluetooth. I don't want Olivia to hear my conversation with Marissa.

"Where are you?" Marissa asks as she answers the phone.

"Olivia's car wouldn't start. I'm taking her to work and then I'll be there."

"Olivia? My cousin, Olivia?"

"Of course. Who else?"

"And you're taking her all the way to work? In Salt Springs?"

"Yes."

Silence greets me. I know what Marissa is like to others. I'm fully aware of the comments and the tantrum she's suppressing for my benefit. She's very good at maintaining her carefully forged façade. She knows our relationship would cease to be if she didn't. For that reason, she doesn't speak until she has her temper under control.

"That's awfully nice of you to do that for her. Just know that I don't expect it. She's related to me, but I would never ask you to go out of your way like this."

"I know you wouldn't. I don't mind. Really."

Another pause.

"All right. I guess I'll see you in a couple hours, then."

"See you soon."

When I lay my phone in the cup holder, I see Olivia watching me.

"Something wrong?"

"I was wondering the same thing. Is she mad?"

"No. Why would she be mad?"

"Do you even *know* who you're dating?"

I can't help but laugh. "She's not all bad. She was fine with it."

"Hmmm."

"Obviously there's no love lost between you two. So why are you living with her?"

I glance at Olivia and I see her face crumble.

"I sound like an ungrateful witch, don't I? And she *is* your girlfriend. I'm so sorry!"

Damn, I've made her feel bad.

"Please don't apologize. It wasn't my intention to make you feel bad. I was just curious how it all came about."

"Marissa didn't tell you?"

"No. She doesn't talk much about it."

"Figures," she murmurs. I act like I don't hear her. But it makes me want to smile. "Well, the roommate I've had for the last two years up and followed her boyfriend to Colorado without telling me. It was time to renew the lease and I didn't have the money to continue it on my own, so I had to make other arrangements. My best friend offered me her couch, but she's getting married next month, so that's just not gonna happen. That left me with the dorms. Until Marissa's father offered to let me stay with her. He isn't charging me as much as I'd have to pay for room and board at school, which is great because that would've been a huge problem for me. I'm on a pretty tight budget, even though Tad pays me really well to bartend." She looks to me, and I nod in understanding. "It doesn't sound like it, but I really am grateful. I've just had a rough week."

"So you bartend?"

"Yep."

"Can I ask why you drive so far when there are probably dozens of bars in the city that would hire you?"

"Tad pays better than any of the places I've checked. He has a lot of girls that call in for their weekend shifts, so he pays me extra to work every weekend. I've worked there for two years and I've known him half my life. He knows I'll always show up."

"I guess it's a good thing I forced you into letting me bring you, then."

She grins at me. It's a cute, sexy little grin that makes me want to kiss her.

And that's not good.

"I guess I owe you one."

"I'm sure I can think of something you can do to pay me back."

Dude, now you're flirting?

Even to my own ears, my comment sounds suggestive. The

sad thing is, it was meant that way. There are literally a dozen things I'd love for her to do for me. Or to me. Or let me do to her.

Her grin widens into a smile. "Just let me know when you think of something, then."

Great! Now she's flirting back!

I should mind. I should be opposed to it. But I'm not. Far from it!

I need to change the subject. "So, I don't know how much my brother pays, but I'm sure he's very competitive. Why don't I talk to Cash about you? He might have an opening."

I see panic on her face. "No!"

"O-kay," I say, a little shocked by her reaction. "May I ask why not?"

She sighs and leans her head back against the headrest, closing her eyes. "It's kind of a long and very embarrassing story."

"Does it have something to do with you taking his clothes off?"

Her head jerks up and she turns wide eyes on me. "Did he say something about it?"

"No, you mentioned it that first morning, remember?"

Her expression calms. "Oh yeah. That's right."

"So just because of one little incident like that, you'd refuse a job offer that would keep you closer to home and probably put more money in your pocket?"

"Well, the more-money-in-my-pocket thing remains to be seen. You don't know how much he pays."

"I can almost guarantee it would be enough to make it worth your while. His club is pretty big."

"Hmmm," she answers again.

"You should at least think about it. Unless you want me to force you again. I could carry you in there, you know."

She looks over at me and smiles. And I want nothing more than to pull over and drag her into my lap.

"On second thought, maybe I'd rather you make me force you."

What the hell are you doing, man?

She picks her head up off the headrest, then cocks it to one side. "Are you flirting with me?"

I shrug. She's very direct. I like that.

"Would you mind if I were?"

"Marissa is my cousin, you know."

"But you can barely stand her."

"That's not the point. I'm not *that* girl."

I look at her. And I don't doubt her for one second. She might think Marissa's a cold bitch, but she would never purposely do anything to hurt her.

"Believe it or not, I know you're not. I'm a pretty good judge of character and I have no doubts you're not *that* girl."

Her brow wrinkles. "Then why are you flirting with me?"

She's serious. She's not smiling or teasing, but she's not judging me, either. She's just curious.

I'm fascinated and, for one second, completely honest with her.

"I can't seem to help myself."

SEVEN

Olivia

How in the world did I let him talk me into this?

I'm standing in front of the main door of Dual. I look long and hard at the sign. I have to smile. Dual. Double. Two. Twins. It appears Cash is cheeky in every aspect of his life. And clever.

Dammit.

It's broad daylight and the parking lot is empty. I'm having serious reservations about what I'm getting ready to do. Nash has pestered me about letting him get me a job at the club since Sunday night when my dad dropped me back at the condo.

Even though it seems that Cash and Nash don't get along very well at all, Nash offered to bring me by and officially introduce me to his brother. Stubborn idiot that I am, I refused to even consider the job. But now that the weekend approaches and I'm dreading going all the way back to Salt Springs to work at Tad's, I'm feeling more optimistic about working for Cash. Unfortunately, Nash had to go out of town again, so now I'm stuck going in alone. And I'm having second thoughts. Especially since the reason I'm most anxious to stick around town on the weekends is to see more of Nash, who is strictly off limits.

You're such a dumbass! Talk about flirting with disaster!

I sigh and shift my weight from foot to foot, debating what to do. I look longingly back at my car, the car that Nash had a mechanic come look at and fix before I even got back home on Sunday. Turns out it was something simple with a spark plug, I think he said. But still . . . He had it fixed.

I sigh.

It's the possibility of seeing more of Nash, of him casually dropping by to check on me, that pushes me in the direction of the door.

I open it and walk into the dark interior. Even in the middle of the day, very little light shines in through the small, high windows.

The bar looks totally different without the wild lights and the wall-to-wall crush of bodies. The high tables are clean and empty, the black floors are polished to a shine, there is some kind of instrumental music pouring softly from the speakers, and the only illumination in the whole room is the backlit liquor display cases behind the bar.

Nash said Cash would be here all day, but I'm beginning to think I should've had him set a specific time. I have no idea where to look for him.

My flip-flops make a hushed flapping sound against my heels as I make my way across the room. I walk to the bar and pull out a stool to sit on, hoping Cash is keeping an eye on the place since the door was open.

I nearly swallow my tongue when Cash pops up from behind the bar. "You must be Olivia."

"Holy mother of hell!" I say, grabbing my chest to still my racing heart.

He laughs. "With a mouth like that, you'll fit right in here."

If I weren't so surprised, I'd probably take exception to that comment. Instead, I laugh.

"You bring out the worst in me. What can I say?"

Cash is wearing a black tank top that perfectly showcases his muscular arms and the interesting tattoo that peeks out on the left side of his chest. I try not to think of him as mouthwatering, but that's the word that keeps going through my head.

Dammit!

He puts his elbows on the bar and leans in closer to me. "That's because you haven't given me the chance to bring out the best in you."

His voice is deep and quiet. His brow is arched, much like it was that first night—in a suggestively challenging way. I feel my pulse pick up.

Good God, he's even hotter than I remember!

Somehow, I'd managed to convince myself that he wasn't as appealing as Nash, that because he's the bad boy of the two, he's less attractive. Sweet Lord, was I wrong!

I try desperately to hang on to my brain and make a better

impression this time. I know I'll only get this one chance to redeem myself.

I smile politely and respond. "Well, that won't be a problem if I start working for you, right?"

He leans back and smiles crookedly. "Already threatening a sexual harassment suit?"

"No, I . . . of course not! I . . . I didn't mean . . . what I actually meant was . . ." In my head, I hear the sound of an airplane falling from the sky at terminal velocity, then crashing into the side of a mountain with a loud explosion.

Shut up, Olivia! Please, just shut up!

"Don't back down now! This was just getting interesting."

I exhale. I'm both relieved and a little irritated.

He's teasing me!

"Are you always this evil?"

"Evil?" he asks, his expression innocent. "Me? Nooooo."

With a grin, he plants his hands flat on the bar and lifts himself onto it, throwing his legs over and hopping down right beside me. I actually squeeze my eyes shut for a second in hopes that the vision of his biceps and triceps straining against his smooth skin won't be permanently etched onto my mind. I think I'm too late, though, because it's all I can see on the backdrop of my lids.

Dammit!

"Nash says you bartend, right?"

My eyes open to his. He's staring down at me, so close I can see the vague line where black pupil stops and nearly black iris begins. Those eyes are amazing!

I see his eyebrows rise, prompting me.

"Pardon?" I ask.

"Nothing. I don't even think it matters. If you're this adorably sexy all the time, no one will care how fast you get them their drinks."

I flush a little at his words. They shouldn't please me. But they do. Quite a bit.

"That won't be a problem."

"What? You being adorably sexy? No, I can see that."

"That's not what I meant. I've been working at one of the busiest sports clubs in Salt Springs for the last two years. I can hold my own behind your bar."

He crosses his arms over his chest and smirks at me. "You think so?"

I feel my spine straightening. "I know so."

"The people that come here want to be served as well as entertained. Think you can handle that, too?"

I'm thinking to myself that I don't even know what that means, but my mouth has already moved on.

"Not a problem."

"So then you won't mind giving me an . . . audition."

His pause gives me a little chill that races down my spine. I clear my throat and reach deep for my bravado. "Audition? What did you have in mind?"

He doesn't answer for a few seconds. Long enough to make me squirm. Long enough for me to think of all sorts of different types of auditions, a couple of which excite me.

Get your mind out of the gutter, Liv! He's off limits!

He laughs. "Nothing *too* creative. I don't want to push my luck with the sexual harassment thing. Yet."

"Are you *trying* to run me off?"

"Oh, come on. You can't tell me you've never worked for someone who's attracted to you. I bet that happens to a girl like you all the time."

I resist the ridiculous grin that's tugging at my lips. I can't let him see that I'm pleased to hear him admit to being attracted to me, especially when *pleased* is code for *I can barely breathe, I'm so excited.*

"A girl like me?" I ask in my calmest manner.

"Yeah, a girl like you." Cash's lids drop down partway over his eyes, making them look like heavy, bedroom eyes, and his voice is like the silk sheets I can imagine him sleeping on. "Feisty, sexy, gorgeous as hell. I bet you've never met a man you couldn't wind around your little finger."

He's watching me like he wants to undress me right where we are—in an empty bar with low light and soft music. And there's a tiny part of me that would love for him to do exactly that.

I snort.

Ohmigod, I *snort*! "Not hardly."

"Yeah, you say that, but I'd bet you could have your way with any guy you want." He cocks his head to one side as he considers me. I get the feeling he's weighing me, assessing me. "But maybe you just don't know it."

"I . . . I . . . I don't know what you mean," I say, hating that my voice sounds so breathless. I don't want Cash to know he affects me at all.

"Hmmm," is all he says. After several more seconds of trying to figure me out, Cash smiles. It's a polite smile that says he's back to business. Well, at least as much as he has been thus far. "So, audition it is. Can you come for a shift tomorrow night?"

I hate to call in at Tad's, but I don't want to quit until I know I have a job here, either. So it's either call in at Tad's or blow off this audition. I don't have much choice.

"Sure. What time should I be here?"

"Seven. That way Taryn can show you the setup before the doors open at nine."

"Sounds good," I say, nodding. Silence stretches between us and I'm at a loss. "Well, I guess I'd better let you get back to your work."

"Aren't you going to ask about money? Nash said that was kind of a thing."

Holy crap! I'm so freakin' bedazzled I forgot to even ask about the pay!

I feel my cheeks get hot. I pray it's too dark for him to notice, and that if he does, he chalks it up to my discomfort with talking about money matters.

"Yes, there is that."

"How about two dollars per hour above what your current employer is paying you?"

My mouth wants to drop open. "Don't you even want to know what that is?"

He makes a face. "Nah. I get the feeling you'll be worth it."

"No pressure there," I mumble.

He laughs again. "Oh, there'll be plenty of pressure. Don't you worry about that. This place is kickin' on the weekends."

I want to remind him I've been here, but I don't want him to be thinking about me undressing him.

Too late.

"And you've only seen the upstairs," he says with a wink.

I should've known I wouldn't get out of here without some reference to that.

"Can we just forget that ever happened?"

His smile is devilish. "Not on your life." He starts backing up, away from me, away from the exit. "I'll see you tomorrow night. Seven o'clock."

"Should I wear something particular? Or . . ."

"I'll send some stuff to your house. Size six, right?"

For some reason, knowing he's checked me out so closely that he can estimate my size makes me feel warm in all sorts of places that I shouldn't feel warm.

"Yes."

He winks again, then turns around and disappears into a barely visible door at the back of the bar.

EIGHT

Cash

I smile as I hear the door bang shut behind Olivia. She's gone.

I hate that I had to cut the interview short, but I can already see that girl's gonna have a way of making me do and say crazy, stupid shit. In a way, I like it. I like *her*.

She's such a contradiction. I can tell she's attracted to me, but she tries not to be. I can tell she's a little shy, but she tries not to let that show, either. And watching her put on a brave face, watching her rise to a challenge, is so damn hot! It makes me want to push her, to see how far she'll go.

I know that sounds perverse, but it's true. Something about her reaction to my taunts gets my juices flowing. All I know is that having her around so much is going to make for some very interesting weekends!

I sit down to type out an email to Marie, who owns the

shop that supplies me with all my uniforms. I can't help but think of what Olivia will look like in the low-slung black jeans and snug black tank top. I don't want my bartenders to look like whores, but I don't mind for them to show a little skin and a little cleavage. It sells more drinks. And, in Olivia's case, it will provide *me* with lots of pleasure.

I'm very much looking forward to tomorrow night. She's already got that cute-'n'-sexy thing going on. Putting her in an element where I can focus on getting her to spread her wings a little will be the most fun I've had in a long time. I'm already thinking of what I can ask her to do for her "audition."

NINE

Olivia

The ring of my cell phone wakes me up. I open one bleary eye and look at the bedside clock. It's four minutes past six. In the morning. Who in the world would be calling me at such an ungodly hour?

I look at the lighted screen of my phone. I don't recognize the number and I consider not answering. The fact that it *is* so early is what makes me reach for it. I always feel a little tingle of alarm when my phone rings at an unusually early or late hour.

"Hello?" I say, my voice hoarse even to my own ears.

"Olivia?"

A shiver runs down my spine. It's Cash. His voice conjures an image of his handsome face, cocky smile, and sexy chest. Instantly, I feel all melty.

"Olivia?" he says again.

No, it can't be Cash. It must be Nash. It's too early for a club owner to be up. Sadly, I'm equally excited by the mental image and prospect of Nash calling me, too.

I am so much more twisted than I ever realized!

"Yes."

A deep rumbly laugh.

So effing sexy!

"It's Nash. I'm sorry to call so early, but I'll be out most of the day and I wanted to see how things went at the club. Did you take the job?"

"It's no bother. Really. I appreciate you checking up on it. Um, actually I have an 'audition' tonight. Whatever that is."

"Ahhh," he says knowingly. "Cash likes for his people to be willing to entertain."

For the first time, I remember that Cash is the one who supplied the stripper, and true horror sets in.

Sweet Lord, I can't strip!

I sit straight up in bed. "Holy hell! He doesn't expect me to strip, does he?"

Another laugh.

"No. Unless you *want* to strip."

"Good God, no!"

"I didn't think so, especially after your first experience at Dual."

There's a smile in his voice.

Cash told him! Dammit!

I think a change of subject is in order. "So what does that mean, then, 'entertain'?"

"Let's just say you can't be shy in front of a crowd. Are you okay with that?"

Yes, I tend to be a little shy, but it's in no way debilitating. And frankly, I'm a little miffed that he might be implying that it is.

"Believe me, Nash, I can do what any of the other girls can do, no problem."

Well, that might not be entirely true. But I'll be damned if I'll ever admit it!

"Then you won't have any problems. With your looks and personality, you'll kill 'em."

His comment pleases me. Even though he's not supposed to notice what I look like. But I'm so glad he does. It means that he's not immune to me, which is actually a bad thing, but one that makes me feel not so alone in my attraction. Still, nothing can ever happen. He's taken.

Dammit.

I hear a muffled beep, like Nash is getting another call.

"Speak of the devil. That's Cash calling now," Nash says. Then he mutters almost absently, "Wonder what he's doing up so early?" I think it's funny that I wondered the same thing. After a couple seconds, he clears his throat and continues. "Well, anyway, good luck tonight. That's all I really wanted to say. Go back to bed. Get your beauty rest. Not that you'll need it."

I find myself smiling like a loon. I feel like giggling, but I quell the urge. "Thanks, I will."

"Sleep well, Olivia."

Even after he hangs up, the skin of my arms and chest is puckered with chills. I love the way he says my name.

How in the world did he get my number? I think randomly.

I lie in my bed for a long time, staring at the ceiling and thinking of Nash. Wondering what it would be like to be staring at his ceiling instead, wherever he's at, lying in bed beside him. My eyes drift closed as I think of him rolling over to cover my body with his, to feel his hips fit between my thighs.

Those are the thoughts that usher me back into sleep.

Dual looks very nearly the same as it did yesterday, only tonight a few more lights are on and there are voices. Two of them, and one is raised in undeniable anger.

"So I get stuck training some newbie? This is such bullshit! I have the most seniority here. He should've at least asked me."

I can see who the voice belongs to—a wisp of a girl with long blond dreadlocks and one arm full of tattoos. She's waving her hands in furious animation, shouting at a young guy who looks about as cool as a cucumber.

"Slow your roll, psycho," he says good-naturedly. I can only see the back of his dark head, but I know he's smiling. I can hear it in his voice. In fact, he sounds like he's trying not to laugh. "He said she's got experience. She probably won't need that much training."

"If she's gonna be working with me, either she'll be the best or I won't work with her."

"You're such a sweet, agreeable beer wench, you know that, Taryn?"

The girl, Taryn, who had turned away to fill up something behind the bar, whirls on him so fast I can hear her dreads slap his face.

"What did you call me?"

The guy tips his head back and laughs. Hard. I fully expect to see the girl go for his eyes, but instead, she surprises me and grins. And just like that, it's over.

"Are you gonna try to get off and go to the concert with me?" she asks congenially.

Their voices drop into a more conversational tone that I can't hear as clearly and feel guilty for listening to. Time to either get the hell out of here or make my presence known. And trust me, it's no easy decision. Just the thought of working with someone like this girl Taryn gives me heartburn.

Before I can give much consideration to backing out, I reach down for every last ounce of bravado I possess, clear my throat, and start making my way toward the bar.

Both heads turn to watch me as I approach. As I get closer, I can see that, although obviously in possession of one hellacious temper, the girl is quite beautiful with her wide almond eyes and full ruby lips. And the guy is . . . wow! He's quite beautiful, too.

He looks exotic. Maybe Hawaiian or Cuban. He has light caramel skin, jet black hair, and eyes to match. And the smile he turns on me? Holy shit.

What is this? The land of misfit models?

I try not to be self-conscious in my outfit. It's not very revealing, at least not uncomfortably so, but I still feel . . . nervous. The pants ride low, showing off a decent-sized square of stomach, and the tank top is probably a size smaller than what I'd normally wear, revealing a healthy shot of cleavage. All in all, it's nothing trashy, but it'll get me plenty of attention, I'm sure. *That's* what makes me nervous.

I don't fill my shirt out nearly as well as Taryn, whose buoyant boobs are undeniably artificial. She's skinny everywhere else, though, which makes me kinda proud of my curves. If there's one thing I've got, it's junk in my trunk.

I smile widely and stick out my hand. "Hi. I'm Olivia. You must be Taryn," I say, addressing the girl first. Evidently, if there's anyone I can expect to have trouble with, it'll be her.

"I would say I've been expecting you, but I just found out I'll be training you, so . . ."

She's prickly, yes, but not overtly hostile. I take that as a good sign and go in like a linebacker. "I'll try my best to catch on quick. Luckily, I have plenty of bartending experience, so . . ." I say, trailing off like she did.

She nods, but her smile is clearly doubtful. "We'll see."

"Great!" I say exuberantly. "I look forward to it." Quickly, I turn to the guy, aiming my hand in his direction. He's still smiling. "Olivia."

"Marco," he says smoothly, his eyes twinkling with mischief. Every now and again you meet someone you just *know* is immediately attracted to you. There is no doubt in my mind that Marco is attracted to me. He's not even trying to hide it. And why would he? There's probably not a female on the planet who could resist the charms of someone like him—dark, hot, easygoing, killer smile. "My night just got a whole lot better."

Oh, he's gonna be a handful!

"Maybe mine did, too," I reply with a playful grin. My ability to flirt with him is the biggest indication that nothing will ever happen between us. It's the guys who tie me in knots, like Nash and Cash, that give me reason to worry.

"Turn that cutesy smile of yours on some customers and maybe you'll do all right, but you still better be able to sling some drinks," Taryn says sharply as she walks away.

Marco makes a shooing motion with his hand and rolls his eyes. "Just ignore her. She's in a constant state of heightened PMS. She gets a little better once the place fills up."

I smile and nod, but I'm thinking, *Oh, thank God!*

"Maybe her dreads are too tight," I mumble.

Marco laughs. "Damn! Beautiful *and* funny. I can't wait to see what else you're hiding behind that sexy smile."

"Nothing as charming as what you've got behind yours, I'm sure."

Marco starts nodding, his smile never faltering. "Oh, yeah. We're gonna get along just fine."

TEN

Cash

I rarely *dread* work, but I usually don't look forward to it quite this much, either. I give the room enough time to fill up and then go out to check on Olivia's progress. I've made a point to give her time to adjust before showing my face. I figure that might make her nervous.

I know she wants me. Or at least I think she does. I just think she doesn't *want* to want me. That alone piques my interest.

I don't mind the cat-and-mouse thing we've got going on. I'm willing to play a little to get her into my bed. I've got good instincts about women most of the time, and my gut tells me she'll be worth the wait.

When I step onto the floor, I look across the ocean of moving heads. My eyes go straight to the bar. To Olivia.

I have a clear shot of her, partly because I stand a couple

inches over the tallest person between us and partly because there is a little bubble of men around her. Already.

She's smiling at a customer as she mixes a rum and Coke. I watch her take his card and run it through the machine at the register, like she's been doing it every day for years.

She's good. And I'm pleased. I would've kept her, anyway, but it's nice to know she's worth it.

Oh, she's worth it, all right.

My mind wants to drift off to visions of laying her out on the bar when the club is empty, of peeling her clothes off and licking her smooth skin. Ruthlessly, I wrangle my thoughts and bring them back to the matter at hand—her audition. She never needs to know that it's unnecessary. She'd be hired regardless. But I'm having her audition, anyway, more for my pleasure than anything else.

I shoulder my way through the crowd, making my way to her end of the long, straight bar. I stop at the edge of the semicircle of guys surrounding her and wait until she looks up and sees me. When she does, I see her pause. It's nearly imperceptible, so much so that I doubt anyone else notices. But I notice. And that's all that matters.

She licks her lips nervously and smiles. I wink at her, just to see what she'll do. She pauses again and her cheeks get red, but then she looks away.

She frowns for a second. I don't think she even realizes she's doing it.

Damn, I love that! She reacts to me even when she doesn't want to.

I don't know why she tries so hard to resist me. I'm not such a bad guy. I'm fit and healthy, a successful business owner, I'm not in debt, and I'm pretty damn good-looking. Or so I hear, anyway.

I move in closer to the bar, leaning one elbow on it as I turn to the group of guys. "So, what's it gonna be, boys? We've got a new bartender to audition."

Cheers go up all around me. Olivia's got a fan base already. She's gonna make me a killing.

I hear terms like *bar dance*, *sing-along*, and *crowd crawl* being tossed around, but then two words rise above the rest and soon everyone has joined in to chant them.

"Body shot! Body shot! Body shot!"

Olivia is watching with interest as her fate is decided.

"Body shot it is!" I shout.

I look at Olivia and raise my hands, palm up. "The bar has spoken." She gives me a nod and a small smile as she wipes her hands on her jeans. "Pick your victim."

She bites her lip as she looks across the bar at all the guys watching her. I know without a doubt each one is wishing they could be the lucky guy, but she's a smart girl. She knows there's more to this "audition" than meets the eye. She's weighing her options and thinking about an appropriate response.

Having worked in a bar before, she has to know that drinking on the job is strictly forbidden, which excludes Marco and Taryn. She probably also knows that engaging in something like this with a customer is frowned on as well. She's thinking it through.

Smart girl.

An audition at my bar is always about finding a way to keep the people happy without breaking any rules. I'm a rule breaker by nature, but I'm strict with my employees. This bar is my livelihood, after all. I can't afford lawsuits, injuries, and brawls.

I watch Olivia as she assesses the situation. When her eyes fall on me, I know she realizes I'm her only viable option. I'm not sure if I see a flicker of excitement cross her face or if it's just my imagination. What I'm certain I see, however, is her reaching for that bravado again. And it's just as sexy as it was before.

She turns to the guys around me and treats them to a beguiling smile. "Think my boss here will man up and do it?"

Some good-natured ribbing begins as I get playful pushes and slaps on the back. There's lighthearted jealousy and lots of encouragement as I nod to Olivia.

I offer my hand across the bar. She looks at it, takes a deep breath, and then slides her fingers over my palm. I help steady her as she puts a knee on the ledge and climbs onto the bar.

"Clear the bar," I say, and all the guys reach for their drinks, making a space for Olivia to lie down. "Marco, one Patrón body shot!" I call down the bar.

He quickly disengages from the girls he's entertaining to pour the shot and bring the salt dish and two lime wedges down to us.

Rather than leaving it, though, he smiles at Olivia. "Stretch out, beautiful. I'll get you ready."

Normally, the bartender would do just as Marco is doing.

But then again, I'm not usually involved. And for some reason, I wanted to prep Olivia.

Olivia lies down and wiggles to get comfortable on the hard surface of the bar.

I smile tightly as I watch him drag one lime wedge across her bare stomach, circling her navel several times. She's looking up at him, grinning. He's looking down at her, practically salivating. I grit my teeth against the little stab of jealousy I feel.

What the hell's that all about?

Anyone will tell you I don't have a jealous bone in my body. There are too many willing women in the world to get all bent out of shape over one. Envy is just not in me.

Not usually.

Marco's taking his sweet time, wetting her skin and sprinkling salt on her. Taryn switches on the body shot music, which is always "Pour Some Sugar on Me" by Def Leppard. It gets the crowd into it and lets everyone know what's going on. I've never paid it much attention, but as far as mood music goes, tonight I'm really feeling it. I'd like to pour something sweet all over Olivia and then take my time licking it off.

I'm about to hurry Marco along when he finally goes to hand her the shot glass and stick the second piece of lime in her mouth. I can't help but grin when Olivia takes the wedge from his fingers and does it herself. Maybe the attraction I see in Marco's eyes goes only one way.

I feel smug.

Olivia turns to look at me, her eyes wide and alert. I bend

to whisper into her ear. "If you're really uncomfortable with this, you don't have to do it."

I hold my breath as I lean back to get her answer, hoping the brave one will win out.

And it does.

Slowly, Olivia shakes her head and wiggles a little closer to me on the bar. Her eyes are sparkling with determination. And challenge. And it makes me jerk in my jeans.

I grin at her. "All right. You asked for it," I say, just loud enough for the guys around me to hear. They cheer me on.

Moving down to stand in front of her waist, I bend and put my tongue against the skin of her stomach. I feel her muscles contract. The salty and sour flavors cause saliva to gush into my mouth, so I close my lips and swallow, kissing her stomach before continuing to lick my way around her navel.

She lies perfectly still as I lap up all the salt. When I'm done, I lift my head just a little and I see her strain toward me. It's a small movement. Probably nothing anyone else even noticed. But I noticed.

Draping one arm across her hips to hold her still, I dip my tongue into her belly button. She twitches beneath me and I could swear I hear her gasp, even above the music.

When I lift my head, my eyes meet hers and in them, whether she would ever admit it or not, is desire. Lots of hot, sweaty, pin-me-up-against-the-wall desire.

Without looking away, I reach for the shot glass and down the Patrón. I see her chest rise with the deep breath she takes as I move toward her head.

Cupping the back of her neck, I pull her face to mine. I wrap my lips around the lime wedge she holds between her teeth and I suck every last drop of juice from it. The thing is, she never once loosens her hold on it. I can't help but wonder if she's imagining the same scenario with a deserted bar and nothing between us but heat.

When I lean back, I notice she looks as . . . bothered as I feel. I think if we *were* alone, she'd have a hard time saying no to anything I wanted to do to her.

Marco interrupts the moment. "Welcome to Dual!"

Again, cheers go up all around. Olivia's smile is a bit vague as she switches gears from our hot encounter to the fact that there's a bar full of guys vying for her attention. But she recovers quickly, taking the lime out of her mouth and holding it up in victory.

She tosses me a cheeky grin and then spins around to jump off the bar and resume her position as an employee behind it. "All right, guys, who needs a refill?"

And just like that, she's in full swing as a bartender at Dual. My only concern now is keeping Marco away from her.

ELEVEN

Olivia

My first thought upon waking is of Cash. Licking my stomach. Tonguing my navel. And then looking so hard into my eyes.

God, I could've devoured him right then and there!

Damn the bad boys!

I blame everything on my inherent weakness for them, because my head tells me I should be looking for someone much more suitable. Someone like Nash.

Nash.

In my head, I even sigh over his name. He's every bit as delicious as his brother. Obviously. They're twins. And even though he's got less of the edge that seems to draw me in like a bee to honey, he's got so many other things I love.

My phone rings. I look at the Caller ID and no name pops up with the number, which means I don't know the caller. I consider not answering, but I'm already awake so I might as well.

"Hello?"

"Good morning," a gruff voice growls at me. Within a fraction of a second, I not only recognize the voice, but I react to it. My stomach flutters in pleasurable excitement.

"Good morning," I return. It's Cash.

"I was hoping to get to talk to you before you left last night."

His comment brings up an unpleasant thought from the previous night. Just before the last of the patrons were herded out of the building, Taryn had disappeared through the same door I'd seen Cash use, and neither had come back out. Marco had shown me how to close up and, when we were done, he offered to walk me to my car, so I let him. I was irritated and had no intention of waiting around for Cash like a puppy dog. Even if he is my employer. It's the principle of the thing. I remember thinking that he's just like all the other bad boys. Fun-loving, exciting, and, ultimately, unfaithful.

Not that it seems he has anyone to be faithful to, but I wouldn't be the least bit surprised if he did.

Shaking off the thoughts, I remind myself that I don't care about Cash. He's my employer and that's it. End of story.

"I didn't want to interrupt you and Taryn," I explain, hating the waspish bite to my tone. I soften it a bit with, "Marco showed me everything I needed to do, anyway. No big deal."

"Marco, huh?"

Is it my imagination or is there some venom in his *voice now?*

"Yeah. He's great."

He *humphs* and then pauses for a second before continuing. "Taryn had some concerns she needed to address with me before tonight, which is why I'm calling you."

I'm relieved. Instantly. And I hate that I am. It irritates me. But more than that, now I'm worried. This call seems ominous.

"Is there a problem?"

"Look, I'm not the type to beat around the bush or to get involved in petty rivalries, so I'm just gonna be straight with you. Taryn isn't particularly interested in training you. She doesn't have a specific reason; she just isn't. I won't tell you what *I* think it is, because it doesn't matter. What matters is that I want you working at Dual. I know you need a specific shift. If she can't work with you, that's her problem and she can find something else that might make her happy."

"So, what does this mean? What are you saying?"

"Well, when given those options, Taryn decided that she'd rather stay. So, I'm leaving your training up to you. If you want Taryn to train you, she will. If not, then I'll do it."

My pulse speeds up just thinking about spending so much time with Cash. And in such close quarters.

"Can't Marco train me?"

There's a protracted pause before Cash answers. When he does, his tone is clipped. "No. That's not Marco's job."

My mind is racing with a thousand thoughts, not the least of which is that it makes me smile to think Cash might be a tad jealous of Marco.

"I don't know what to say. I mean, I don't want Taryn to think I'm backing down from her. I'm not going to let her run me off. But at the same time, I don't want to put her in a bad position if she's got a problem with me."

"Her job is not to like you, it's to train you. You aren't putting her in a bad position."

My hesitation is minimal. Regardless of my feelings on the issue with Taryn, I know it won't bode well for me if I let Cash train me. I just don't trust myself around him. Not completely, anyway.

"Then I'll let her train me."

"Okay. But if she gives you a hard time, I want you to come to me immediately."

"I will," I agree, having no intention of doing any such thing. No, I'll have to sort out things with Taryn on my own. We'll either learn to get along or learn to work with someone we hate.

I drag a hand through my tangled hair. I hope it's the former rather than the latter. Working with someone who hates me will be stressful in a big, big way.

"She's asked off for tonight, so you won't have to work again until next weekend. Unless you want to pick up an extra shift Wednesday night when she works."

Actually, I need the money. And my classes don't start until eleven o'clock on Thursday, so I could probably swing that, as long as it doesn't become a habit.

"Wednesday's good. I can do that."

"Good," he says. I think I hear a smile in his voice. I'm glad he didn't take it personally that I don't want to be trained specifically by him.

I bet his ego is so big he didn't give it a second thought.

"Well, if there's anything you need, give me a call. I've always got my cell phone with me."

"How did you get my number, anyway?"

"Some asshole named Nash."

"Asshole?"

"Yeah, asshole. Don't tell me you don't think he's an asshole!"

I laugh uncomfortably. "Um, no I don't think he's an asshole. He's always been nice to me."

"Of course he has. You're gorgeous. What man wouldn't be nice to you?"

"Plenty."

"Assholes, all of them," he teases.

"They're assholes, too?"

"Yep."

"Is everyone an asshole today?"

"Yep," he repeats. "Word-of-the-day toilet paper."

I laugh, genuinely this time. "Is that right?"

"Yep. You don't even want to know what yesterday's word was."

"I'm sure I don't. It would probably make my ears bleed."

His voice drops into a lower, softer range. "No, but it would probably make you blush."

I pause. My face feels warm, but pleasantly so. It occurs to me that no matter how much I avoid him, no matter how wrong I know he is for me, he is going to be nearly impossible to resist.

Dammit!

"Enjoy your day, Olivia. I'll see you on Wednesday."

With that, he hangs up, leaving me lying bonelessly on my bed, lost in thoughts of what it would be like to stop fighting it.

I hear voices as soon as I get out of the shower, which is unusual. Marissa's screech is easily and disturbingly identifiable. The raised voice that surprises me, however, belongs to Nash. I creep to the door and crack it the tiniest bit, turning my head and pressing my ear to it.

You are a shameless, creepy eavesdropping hussy.

I stifle a giggle. Apparently I don't cut myself any slack. I pulled out the hussy card.

"You can't just spring something like this on me at the last minute! I already made plans and I don't even have a new dress!" I can tell she's still trying to keep her calm, which is a testament to how much she likes and, therefore, tries to deceive Nash. I'm not sure how much she's actually deceiving him, though. It would be interesting to see how long he'd stick around if she started showing her true colors.

"If I'd known I would be back, I would've said something sooner. I wanted to surprise you." Nash's voice is raised only enough to speak over Marissa's loud whining.

"Well, now what am I supposed to do? I can't cancel on Daddy. He's already—"

"It's not a big deal," Nash offers soothingly. "I can take someone else."

There's a long pause filled with enough tension for me to perceive it through a mostly closed door.

Back up, Nash! She's about to blow!

"Who did you have in mind?"

Her voice is like ice. I wonder if Nash knows that sound and what it means.

"I didn't have anyone particular in mind, as I had no idea you wouldn't be able to go. I'm sure I can find someone last minute, though. No need to worry."

I almost laugh out loud. No need to worry? I bet Marissa is fuming.

I can almost smell the smoke from her overworked brain as she tries to think of someone who will be zero competition for her, someone who is trustworthy, but also someone who is enough of a loser not to already have plans on such short notice.

"What about Olivia? I'm sure she'd be happy to go, especially since you've done so much for her."

I know my mouth is wide open and there is a look of grave insult on my face. I can feel it.

Ohmigod! I'm the loser!

"I appreciate the suggestion, but she works weekends, doesn't she?"

"If she took the job with Cash, who knows what her schedule will be?"

"Well, I'm not waking her up to ask her. I think she worked last night, didn't she?"

"Yes, but she won't mind. I'll ask her."

I hear Nash start to say something, but the way it's cut off makes me think Marissa has already walked off. I close the door silently and haul ass to the bathroom, as though I've just gotten out of the shower, which I technically have.

"Olivia?" Marissa calls, knocking once loudly and then entering. She doesn't even wait for me to give her permission.

I bite back a snarl.

Witch!

"In here," I call sharply.

The door is cracked and I see her practically stomp across the room. She pushes the door open. There's a nasty look on her face. She wastes no time with niceties. "Do you have to work tonight? If not, I need you to go to an art exhibition with Nash. You owe him."

It's just like Marissa to jump right in with the heavy artillery, like guilt and extortion.

I'm so proud to be related to the devil's mistress.

Carefully suppressing the urge to snort, I answer her.

"As a matter of fact, I'm off tonight. I can't go, though. I'm sorry, but I don't have anything to wear to a fancy function like that."

She brushes me off with a wave of her hand. "You can wear something of mine. I'm sure we can make do."

I'd just heard her complain about not having had time to buy a new dress for the event, yet she's perfectly content to send me in . . . whatever.

"As long as Nash doesn't care what I look like . . ."

Marissa laughs in her demeaning little way. "Olivia, I'm sure Nash won't give you a second thought."

I'm gonna be honest. I see red. Red, dammit! And it's in this very moment that I decide I'm going to knock everyone's socks off, especially Nash's. Marissa will rue the day . . .

Even if I have to pull a *Pretty in Pink* and sew my own eff-ing dress in seven minutes flat.

All this is taking place internally. On the outside, I smile sweetly at Marissa. "Well, in that case I'd be happy to."

She turns around and walks away without so much as a *thank you* or *kiss my ass*. When I hear her tell Nash that I'll go and that she'll do her best to make sure I'm presentable, I can't help but wonder if I could get away with stabbing her cold, cold heart with an ice pick.

For that, I might win the Nobel Peace Prize. Or, bare minimum, a call from the Vatican, thanking me.

This time, I don't bother to hide my snicker.

TWELVE

Nash

As I wait for Olivia to come out of her bedroom, I can't help but feel a little ashamed. I shouldn't be looking forward to spending the evening with her as much as I am.

Yet I am. And there's just no denying it.

"Nash?" I hear Olivia call. I turn toward her bedroom. I can see the door from where I'm standing in the living room. It's cracked just enough for me to hear her but not see her.

"Yes?"

"Promise me that if I'll embarrass you in this dress, you'll just go without me. It won't hurt my feelings. I swear."

"Olivia, it doesn't matter what—"

"Promise me right now or I'm not coming out at all."

She's stubborn? Huh. I wouldn't have guessed that. But actually, I kinda like it.

I laugh. "Okay, fine. I promise that if I think you'll embarrass me, I'll go without you."

The door closes and then there's a long pause before it swings all the way open. What I see takes my breath.

Marissa is taller than Olivia. Thinner, too. But Olivia is curvier. Much curvier. And every single one is displayed to absolute perfection in the dress she's wearing.

I think I've seen Marissa in it before, and she looked great. But not great like this.

The material is some kind of thin, almost sheer stuff in dark red. It flutters in the air that stirs as the door comes to a rest against the stopper with a muffled thump. Olivia stands still and lets me appraise her before she starts toward me. I clench my jaw to keep my mouth from dropping open as I watch her. The wispy cloth clings to her body as she walks, outlining her form perfectly. She might as well be nude.

Holy mother, I wish she were.

I shake off the thought, knowing I can't go forward tonight thinking things like that.

Think with the big head, man! Think with the big head!

She glides to a stop in front of me, all grace and luscious skin. Her bare chest and shoulders glow in the low light. I want to touch her, caress her, so much so that I ball my fingers into tight fists to keep them to myself.

"You look beautiful." My voice sounds strained, even to my own ears.

Her face falls. "It's too tight, isn't it? I'm wearing taller heels to make the length right, but there's nothing I can do about the rest." I can see that she's genuinely distressed, which makes me want to smile, although I don't. That would be the wrong thing to do in front of an upset woman. "Marissa is so much thinner than me," she says, one of her hands fluttering as she talks. "And I just don't have anything that—"

I reach out and take her spastic hand, pressing the forefinger of my free hand to her lips. "Shhh." She stops talking immediately. Yes, I could've shut her up a hundred different ways without touching her, but I figure this is better than kissing her, which is what I really want to do.

Good God, how I want to kiss her!

It takes me a few seconds to focus on something other than the way her lush lips part just a little. It would be so easy to slide my fingertip between them, to feel the heat of her mouth, the wetness of her tongue.

I'm both surprised and irritated that I feel my tuxedo pants shrink a size in the crotch. I'll have to be extra careful with this girl. I can't remember the last time someone so thoroughly tested my restraint.

Actually, yes I can. It was Libby Fields in her tight little dress at the homecoming dance in the ninth grade. I thought for sure if she sat in my lap and wiggled her ass one more time, I was going to explode like Mount Saint Helens.

I didn't, of course. But it was close. And this girl—this tiny, curvaceous, engaging, walking, talking contradiction—is working her way up to Libby Fields's position very quickly, which is really saying something since I'm twenty-five, not fourteen.

I clear my throat. "Please don't say another word. You look beautiful. In Marissa's wildest dreams, she could never fill out that dress the way you do. I'll be the envy of every guy in the whole damn place." I smile to further make my point.

Although her brow doesn't smooth entirely, I know she's feeling better when she grabs my wrist and pulls my hand away. I can see the slight curve of her lips where she's holding in a smile.

"Really?"

"Really."

"Really really?"

"Really really. Just remember, tonight you're mine."

It worries me how much I like the sound of that, the thought of that.

Her grin fully forms and she releases my wrist to salute me. "Sir, yes, sir."

I love how playful she is. Such a nice change from Marissa, who's always . . . well . . . who's just *not*.

"Now *that's* what I'm talkin' about," I say with a nod. "A woman who knows her place is beneath me. Oh, wait. That didn't sound right," I tease.

She laughs. "I'm beneath no man!" she replies harshly. Then, with a mischievous quirk to her mouth, she adds, "At least not without dinner and a drink first."

"Ohhhh, so that's how it's gonna be! Because there's a McDonald's right across the street."

I offer her my arm and she curls her fingers around the inside of my elbow. I know it's ridiculous and juvenile, but I flex my bicep, hoping she notices.

"Is that all it takes to get you to, ahem, come to attention?" she asks, suggestively sliding her eyes over me.

"I'm a twenty-five-year-old completing an internship at one of the most influential law firms in all of Atlanta. McDonald's would never do it for me." I stop at the door and open it, gesturing for her to precede me. "But, now, a look like the one you just gave me . . ."

Her cheeks turn a delicate pink and she drops her eyes shyly. It makes me want to tear that dress off her with my teeth.

"Colonel, just what is it you're insinuating?"

"Colonel? A salute like that and all I get is a *Colonel*?"

"I don't know. Have you earned enough stripes to be a general?"

We stroll leisurely to my car. "Depends on how you think someone earns their stripes." Two little dimples pop out on either side of her mouth where she's trying to control her smile.

"Oh, I guess the same way most guys earn their stripes," she says, swinging the red purse attached to her wrist, trying to act nonchalant.

"Baby, if that's your definition, I'd be a four-star general."

She bursts into laughter. I can tell she wasn't expecting me to say that. But I'm so glad I did. Hearing her laugh is like listening to the best kind of symphony.

I'm a little disappointed when we reach the car. I could really just walk and talk and tease her all night long.

THIRTEEN

Olivia

The silence in the car is only slightly tense. Well, maybe *tense* is the wrong word. For me, it feels . . . charged. Sexually charged. I wonder if Nash feels the same way.

Maybe he doesn't. Maybe he flirts with all the girls like this.

I think on that for a second. The prospect is both disappointing and aggravating. But I honestly don't think that's the case. It could just be my ego talking, but I don't think he's like that with just anybody.

At least I hope not.

For some reason, Nash seems like the faithful sort.

I'd be genuinely surprised if he's ever cheated on Marissa.

I bet he's an actual good guy. The kind that I desperately need in my life. The thing of it is, he'll never be mine because he's a good guy. By nature alone, a good guy would never cheat on his girlfriend, hence the impossibility of anything happening between Nash and me. Even if they were to break up, he'd probably be too nice a guy to hurt her like that, by dating her cousin.

As Shawna would say, that sucks major ass!

"Did you solve it?"

Nash's deep, heavenly voice interrupts my troubled thoughts.

"Solve what?"

"World hunger."

I know I must be looking at him like he's sprouted wings or a third eye. He looks from the road to me a couple of times before he starts laughing.

"Yes, in case it isn't apparent at this point, I'm completely lost."

"So it would appear," he teases with a grin. "I just meant that you were thinking awfully hard. Is everything okay?"

I lean my head back against the padded leather headrest and I stare at Nash's handsome profile. With his hair combed smoothly to the side, unlike his brother's messed-up 'do, and his summer-tan skin, he looks like James Bond in his tux. And I fell victim to his charms as if he really were the dashing MI6 agent.

He's got me shaken and stirred.

"You belong in a tux, you know that?" He frowns over at me but smiles. I straighten my head and face the windshield. "Ohmigod, could I be any more random?"

What has gotten into you?

He chuckles. "Actually, I think the answer to that is yes."

"You know me well, Bond."

He chuckles again. "Bond? As in James Bond? Where did that come from?"

I turn my head to look at him again. Immediately it gets all fuzzy with hormones.

"Um, I was, uh, I was thinking about being shaken and stirred." He looks over at me and quirks one brow. "I mean I was thinking how well you could probably shake and stir something."

Ohmigod, somebody stop me!

"I mean, how well you could probably shake and stir a drink. Not me." I snort.

Ohmigod, I just snorted!

"You were?" His mouth curves into a sexy grin. With that brow raised and those lips curled up at the corners, he looks exactly like his brother. Like the twins that they are.

I just stare at him, quite embarrassingly—again—for several seconds before my wits return and I begin to chastise myself.

What the hell is wrong with you? Why don't you just have him pull over so you can climb into his lap?

FYI, that's the wrong kind of thing to think in an effort to settle hot-and-bothered thoughts. That visual sends me into another brief catatonic state as I fantasize about riding in the driver's seat of Nash's car. With Nash still in it.

After several seconds, I remember that he'd said something. "Um, what?" I ask, literally shaking my head to get back some focus.

Nash frowns. "Olivia, are you all right?"

I sigh and turn to face straight ahead again.

Note to self: Do not expect coherent thought to be possible when staring at Nash. Motor skills may be impaired as well. Take necessary precautions.

I almost snicker when I picture myself putting on a helmet, knee pads, and a mouth guard every time Nash enters the room.

Then I think of what I could do in the knee pads . . .

Gahhhhh!

I'm pretty relieved when Nash slows and guides the car into the parking lot of the art gallery. Even though there are no appreciable signs indicating the nature of the establishment, I know that's where we're at. I Googled it before we left so I'd know a little bit of what to expect. I'd hate to fall down some unforeseen stairs or something. I need zero help making a fool of myself in front of this guy.

As the valet pulls away from the curb in the BMW, Nash offers me his arm again and leads me into the gallery. My first impression as I look around at all the artificially tanned skin, medically enhanced figures, and bottle-blond heads is that I've stumbled into Barbie's mansion. Only the black-and-white version, as everyone is in black formal attire. But that's not the only thing gone awry in this Barbie-fied alternate universe. There are no Kens! I see only nerdy, ugly, or just plain old men on most of the women's arms. That's when I realize this must be a trophy wife convention instead.

I look down at my own red-clad, curvaceous physique and then back up at the mostly monochromatic room. As I'm debating running for the exit, Nash leans down to whisper at my ear.

"Is something wrong?"

"I feel like the only splash of color in an abstract painting."

"You *are* the splash of color. But there's nothing wrong with that."

I look at him. He's smiling. It appears to be genuine. He doesn't seem embarrassed by my appearance. I can only hope he's not.

Mentally, I put on my big-girl panties. If he's not bothered, there's no reason for me to be. Right? Right. I take a deep breath. "All right, then. Let's go."

The farther we make our way into the room, the more heads turn in our direction. Most of the men seem to be appreciative of my attire. But the women? Eh . . . not so much.

Nash stops here and there to speak to several couples. It's obvious he's here on business. Besides the perfunctory compliments to the women, he mainly addresses the men. He makes polite chitchat, but there's lots of measuring up going on. Thankfully, he seems to be getting nods of approval left and right.

Why do you even care? It's not like his career or what his peers think should matter to you.

But it does.

Unfortunately, after about twenty minutes, the gloves start coming off. Or should I say that the claws start coming out. And it all begins with a girl who knows Marissa.

"Nash, where's your better half?" the girl I've dubbed Catty Barbie asks. She looks me up and down with a thinly veiled sneer that says she thinks I might've eaten his better half.

"Last-minute change of plans. I'll be sure to tell her you asked about her."

"Please do," she says, not taking her eyes off me. "And who might this little peacock be?"

Peacock? Are you kidding me?

"This is Marissa's cousin, Olivia."

"It's a pleasure, Olivia." It's so not a pleasure, her look says. "Interesting choice for the evening." She nods her imperious head at me.

"His better half chose it," I reply with a super bright smile, wishing the floor would open up and swallow me.

Her collagen-filled lips turn up in a smirk. "Nice."

Nash clears his throat. "I'll tell Marissa to give you a call," he says to Catty Barbie before he turns to her mate. "Spencer, I'm sure we'll talk next week."

Spencer nods to Nash, then smiles at me. His expression says he's sorry that his "better half" isn't better at all, more like toxic instead. I smile in return, thinking I hope showers with her are worth it because I see only misery in his future.

I'm glad Nash doesn't mention the interaction as we move on to the next couple. This pair is every bit as misfit as the previous one. This guy is so dorky-looking, all he really lacks are black-rimmed glasses with tape over the bridge piece and a pocket protector for his tux. And the girl? I'm pretty sure he got her from a movie set where the music sounds like *bow chicka bow wow*. That or she's inflatable.

I think to myself that there's no way these two are going to be nasty. They look so comical themselves, surely they won't throw stones.

But they do. Big ones.

In my head, I dub this one Bimbo Barbie. My assessment of her is only further reinforced when she starts laughing at me the instant we stop in front of them.

"Oh my gawd! Somebody didn't get the memo."

She doesn't even try to keep her voice down. My mouth drops open and my cheeks sting a little when, from the corner of my eye, I see several heads turn in our direction. I can almost feel judgmental eyes burning their way through my brightly colored dress.

I say nothing and make no move to acknowledge her in any way other than to smile, a smile I hope belies my growing humiliation.

Still, Nash doesn't speak. And I'm grateful. I'd likely burst into tears.

We move on to the next couple. And the next. And the next. Each gets progressively worse.

Just when I think there isn't a more rude person left in the room, I meet another one. I shall call her Vapid Barbie.

"Where did you get that dress?"

My stomach drops into my shoes. I want nothing more than to run and hide. After I hunt down Marissa and strangle her with her own dress, of course.

To make matters worse, I feel tears prick the backs of my eyes. I blink quickly and force my lips up into another smile.

It's when I feel Nash stiffen at my side that anger makes an appearance. It's bad enough that they're doing this to me, but Nash has to work with some of these people!

I don't bother to stifle the sharp reply that comes to my tongue. "I stole it from a homeless person," I say, straight-faced. "She was lying right beside the stripper who gave you yours."

Her expression is blank for several seconds before my meaning sinks in. Then her face turns red and her glossy lips drop into a nice big O of shock.

For one second, I'm satisfied. Seeing her speechless makes me feel a teensy bit better. But then I remember the guy at my side. The one I wanted to make a good impression for.

Guilt hits me in the face like a bucket of ice-cold water. And I feel sick.

I smile sweetly at Vapid Barbie and her clueless mate. "Pardon me while I find the ladies' room." To Nash I whisper, my heart in my eyes, "I'm so sorry."

And I make my escape.

I search the hostile environment for the universal signs of a restroom. When I spot the little silhouette of a girl in a dress, I practically run for it. I don't, of course, mainly because I'd probably trip and fall and give everyone an even bigger laugh. But I do walk very, very quickly.

In the bathroom, I keep my head down and make a beeline for the solitude of a stall. Once inside it, I close the door, lean back against it, and let the tears flow.

I'm so embarrassed. And so angry. And so embarrassed again. And for them to be so nasty in front of Nash . . .

My God, those girls make Marissa's vicious bite feel like butterfly kisses! No wonder Nash doesn't mind her.

My tears turn bitter—bitter at them for humiliating me, bitter at me for caring about someone I can never have, and bitter at the reality of how ill-suited I am for a guy like that.

After several more minutes of wallowing in self-pity and the cruel why-oh-whys of life, I exit the stall. I know if I don't get back soon, someone will think I'm in here blowing up the toilet. And that's the last thing I need.

No, you horrid ho-bags, my stress response is not intractable irritable bowel syndrome!

Thankfully the bathroom is empty, so I get to clean up my ravaged makeup and tear-streaked face in peace. I run a few paper towels under the cold water and hold them to my eyes like compresses, hoping they'll reduce the swelling. All they manage to do is make my already-wet lashes clump together.

I shake my head at my reflection. The only thing I can do at this point is go back out there with my head held high and a smile on my face and try to finish the rest of the night without incident.

You can do this, Liv. You can do this.

I almost add *for Nash*, but even in my head, it sounds stupid and presumptuous. He's not mine to care for. No matter how much I wish he were.

I take a deep breath and fling open the door to head back into the viper den. But I don't get very far. I stop dead in my tracks when I see Nash leaning against the wall right outside the ladies' room. His legs are crossed casually at the ankle, as his arms are crossed casually over his chest. His smile is faint. And sad.

I say nothing. I don't know what to say. I fidget with the little wristlet purse dangling against my palm.

Finally, he straightens and steps toward me. He doesn't stop until he is mere inches from me, forcing me to tilt my face up just to maintain eye contact.

He brushes his thumb over the ridge of my cheekbone at the corner of my eye. I wonder briefly if I missed a streak of mascara.

"I'm so sorry," he whispers, closing his eyes as if in pain. His face is etched with regret and it tugs at my heart.

"Don't be. You can't control other people. I just hope I haven't embarrassed you too badly, or ruined any important business connections you were hoping to make."

"I don't care about business connections. Not at this cost."

"But you should. That was the whole point of coming tonight. It shouldn't be ruined by some random girl who's too much of a misfit to bring to functions like this."

"You're not the misfit. I am. I'm the one masquerading as something I'm not," he says pensively.

"Not being like them is a good thing, but you have to play by their rules. It's part of the game. It's part of who you are and what you do."

"It may be part of what I do, but it's not part of who I am. I'm not this guy. Not really. This," he says, tugging on the lapel of his tux, "serves a purpose. It's a means to an end. Nothing more."

I frown. "A means to what end?"

Nash's inky eyes bore holes into mine and, for a second, I think he's going to tell me something. But then he changes his mind and smiles another small smile.

"Nothing I want to get into right now. Come on," he says, reaching down to take my hand. "Let's get out of here."

Nash leads me to the door and we leave without a backward glance.

He doesn't say another word as he helps me into his car, starts it up, and heads toward the northern edge of the city. I don't ask where he's taking me; I really don't care. I'm just glad to be in his presence and away from all those other people. Anything else is just gravy.

I'm a little surprised when I start seeing the buildings grow taller as Nash weaves his way through the streets of downtown. He slows and pulls into a parking garage, waving a card in front of an electronic eye. A gate lifts and he drives through. He slides into the first available spot and cuts the engine.

Still, he doesn't say a word. He helps me out of the car and leads me to an elevator.

Still, I don't ask questions. I'm sort of excited and very curious to see where he's taking me. I shouldn't be. Because he's not mine. But I am.

He flashes his card before another red eye then punches the button for the twenty-fourth floor. The doors close with a hushed swish. We ride smoothly upward until the doors open into a luxurious, dimly lit reception area. Directional lighting sparkles like thousands of diamonds in the gold lettering that reads "Phillips, Shepherd, and Townsend."

We're at the law firm where he works. With Marissa. And my uncle. Who's a partner. He's the Townsend in Phillips, Shepherd, and Townsend.

I want to ask why we're here, but again, I don't. He takes my hand and tugs, leading me out of the elevator car into the quiet of the empty office. We make our way across to another, smaller bank of elevators. We go up two more floors, but when the doors open this time, it's to a breathtaking view of the brightly lit skyline of Atlanta.

I gasp. I can't help it. I've never seen such a beautiful sight. It's like a postcard. Only real.

I weave my way around groupings of expensive outdoor furniture until I reach the wall that surrounds the rooftop. The warm breeze teases the hair at my temples as I look out at the Bank of America building across the way.

"Up here, people like that don't exist," Nash says quietly as he comes to stand beside me. He's so close his shoulder is brushing mine. I fight the urge to lean against him.

I can feel warmth from his body radiating toward me, teasing me with its enticing heat. I shiver in response.

"Are you cold?" he asks, turning toward me to run the backs of his fingers up and down my upper arm, as if testing the temperature of my skin. "Here," he says, taking off his jacket and draping it over my shoulders. The jacket is warm and heavy and smells just like Nash, like whatever cologne or soap he uses. I figure it must be called *delicious*, maybe by Armani or some other fancy designer. It almost makes my mouth water. "Is that better?" He wraps his arm around me, too, as if to ensure I won't be cold. Of course, I won't complain. Even if I were sweating, I wouldn't complain.

"That's much better, thank you."

We stand in silence for so long I finally begin to get uncomfortable. But just when I start to rack my brain for things to say, Nash speaks.

And drops a nice little bomb.

FOURTEEN

Nash

"My father's in prison. For murder."

Way to just blurt it out, idiot!

I don't know why I feel so compelled to tell Olivia all my dirty little secrets, but I do. Maybe it's because she feels like the misfit. I can relate to that. In a world where appearances and reputation mean everything, I have to work extra hard to make sure that everything I say and do is above reproach. It was a nearly impossible feat to overcome, outlive, and outdistance myself from my father and his imprisonment, but I did it. After years and years of hard work and kissing all the right asses, I finally did it. And now I'm one step closer to my goal.

After what feels like a freakin' eternity of silence, I look down at her. She's looking up at me, her lips slightly parted in shock. Her bright green eyes, dark in the dim light, are focused sharply on mine. But the thing I notice most isn't what's in them—surprise, disbelief, curiosity, maybe a little pity—it's what's not. Judgment. Disdain. Horror. None of the things I've so often seen in people's eyes when I've had to tell them my story.

Now I want to kiss her even more.

Damn you! You just get more and more appealing.

"What? No running away, screaming?" I say, unable to keep the slight trace of bitterness from my voice.

She surprises me with a grin and a dubious look. "I think we've clearly established that I'm nothing like the people you normally associate with."

I laugh. And it's genuine. "Yeah, I guess we have."

She turns toward me. The only thing on her face now is interest. Simple curiosity. I'm glad to see that trace of pity gone. Of the many things I'd like to have from this girl, pity is nowhere on the list.

"Wanna talk about it?"

I shrug. "It doesn't bother me as bad as it used to. It feels more like part of my past now than anything else."

"It must be more than that for you to want to tell me about it."

Perceptive. She's as smart as she is beautiful. And probably doesn't think she's either one.

"Maybe. I don't know. I don't even know why I brought it up." I look out at the twinkling city lights. Now I feel like a fool for mentioning it.

"But you did. Now you have to tell me or I'll be forced to think you're cruel and sadistic."

"Maybe I am."

She narrows her eyes at me, sizing me up. "Nah. I don't believe it. Besides, isn't there some law against cruel and unusual punishment? You can't be a lawyer and a lawbreaker at the same time."

I chuckle at her logic. I can't help but wonder what she'd think if she knew the truth. "People do it all the time."

"But you aren't 'people.' You're the guy who's getting ready to put me out of my misery."

"Misery, huh?" I ask, quirking one brow at her.

I know my smile probably gives away the direction my thoughts have taken, and Olivia manages to surprise me again when she immediately jumps in to play along.

"Yes, misery," she agrees with a smile. "You're not the kind of guy to leave a girl hanging, are you?"

Although she seems sweet and innocent and shy, at times she seems ready to participate in a much more intimate and dangerous game. I know I shouldn't be thinking about games or misery or anything else concerning Olivia Townsend.

But damn if I'm not!

Dark and dirty things come to mind, things like how much pleasure I'd get from putting her in misery. But not the bad kind of misery. No, I want Olivia in the kind of misery that makes her sweat and writhe, and then beg me to come inside her.

I feel the need to resituate inside my pants, and I remind myself that I'm drifting onto dangerous ground. My mind understands that, but looking down into Olivia's face, at her sparkling eyes and lush lips, I can't for the life of me get that through to any other body parts.

"Only if that's what she likes," I say, reaching out to pick up a long black lock of hair from Olivia's shoulder. The strand feels like silk between my fingers. So does her skin against the back of my hand. "What do you like, Olivia?"

I think I see her chest rise as she catches her breath. Maybe she'll be the one to throw on the brakes. God knows I'm not going to. I might regret it later, but right now I'm not thinking about anything but what it would be like to see Olivia without that red dress.

Her eyebrow arches. I don't know if it's really in acceptance of my challenge or if that's just what I'm hoping. But then she licks her lips and drops her chin a little, looking up at me from beneath her lashes.

She's coy. But not on purpose. It's just the way she is. And it's an even bigger turn-on.

"You mean you don't know? I figured a four-star general would know all sorts of things the rest of us didn't."

"Maybe I just like to do my own recon."

"And what does that consist of?"

I know I should stop while I still can. Only I can't.

"I like to use all my senses to get a good lay of the land."

"Lay of the land?" she asks, the corners of her mouth dimpling.

"Of course," I reply. "So I can plan my attack."

"Recon? For an attack? Do tell."

"First I start with touch." I reach out and brush one dimple with my fingertip, then slowly drag it inward, across her pouty bottom lip. "Touch is invaluable. The texture of the terrain tells me how . . . aggressive my attack needs to be. Some places require a much more delicate approach than others."

"I see," she says softly, her warm breath tickling my finger. "What else?"

"Smell," I say, sliding my hand into her hair to hold it back as I bury my face in the lightly scented skin of her neck. "A certain scent can tell me if I'm heading in the right direction. Something sweet. Something . . . musky," I murmur.

I hear her gasp when I gently bite the flesh beneath her ear. "And hearing," I whisper. "Sometimes the softest sounds, even a moan can tell me a great deal about how close I am to attaining my goal."

I feel her hands latch onto my forearms. Her fingernails are biting into my skin through my shirt. All I can think about is how I want to feel them on the skin of my back instead.

Her breath is coming fast and shallow in my ear. "What else?" she pants.

I lean back and look down into her face. Her lids are heavy over her dazzling eyes and her cheeks are flushed with everything that's happening between us. She doesn't want to stop, either. There's no doubt in my mind.

"Taste."

Her eyes flicker to my mouth and back again. "And what do you taste?"

"Everything. I want to taste everything."

If I ever stood a chance of resisting her, it evaporates the instant she leans into me. So does every last ounce of finesse that I'm normally capable of. The kiss that should've started out slow starts out like a forest fire. The first taste of her tongue consumes me.

And I'm lost.

My hands are in her hair and my mouth is devouring hers. I give no thought to where I am or the girlfriend whose father I work for. I can't think past how badly I want to be inside the tight, hot body of the girl in my arms.

But why? Why do I want her so bad?

No answer comes to mind. All thought seems to shut down when she wraps her arms around me and I feel those fingernails dig in.

I groan into her mouth and I hear her purr in response. I tug on her hair, maybe a little more roughly than I intend, and her kiss turns ravenous. She leans into me, like she can't get close enough. I turn her around and press her back to the wall. My body is plastered to her length. I can feel every hard inch of me sinking into every soft inch of her. It's the clothes between us that bring me up from the kiss.

I lean back to look at her. Her eyes are dark and her lips are swollen. I can hear sanity knocking at the door, but I ignore it when she leans slowly forward, stretching up on her tiptoes, to bite my lower lip.

"Oh my God," I groan, diving back into the kiss. Olivia meets me right where we were. No reservations.

Without breaking contact with her lips, I bend to pick her up and carry her to one of the chaise longues away from the elevator doors. I lay her on it, stretched out full length, and I straighten to look down at her.

Her knees are slightly bent, giving me a sneak peek at her slim ankles. My attention doesn't stray from there. Dropping to my knees, I press my lips to the top of her foot, pushing the material of her dress up as I make my way to her calf.

My palm skates lightly over her smooth skin, pushing her dress along, as I lick and kiss a trail to her knee, then to the inside of her thigh. She spreads her legs the tiniest bit.

An invitation.

I graze the tender skin with my teeth as the tips of my fingers ascend to brush her damp panties. I hear her gasp. I get hard in anticipation of hearing the noises she'll make when I'm driving my body into hers.

It's when she stiffens that I realize something's wrong. I lift my head and my eyes meet her very alert ones.

I'm confused when I see them fill with tears.

"What's wrong, Olivia? Did I hurt you?"

I didn't think I was rough . . .

She shakes her head. "No, it's just . . . I just . . . we can't do this."

As much as I hate to admit it, I know she's right. Marissa is too important in my plans to mess things up now. And Olivia is way too nice a girl for me to drag her into my crazy life.

With a sigh, I rest my forehead against her knee.

FIFTEEN

Olivia

"You're right," I hear Nash murmur. Then, when he picks up his head, he says more firmly, "You're right. Please accept my apology."

He seems stiff and . . . distant. And it's making an already uncomfortable situation much, much worse. I sit up and reach for his arm before he can stand up and move away.

"No, wait. Don't do that. It was my fault. I was flirting with you, knowing that you're taken. Very taken. It's as much my fault as yours. Can't we just sort of forget about it? Not let things get weird?"

He watches me with those intense eyes for several seconds before he speaks. And when he does, I'm relieved. "Sure," he says, getting to his feet and offering me his hand. I slip my fingers inside his, and he squeezes them lightly and pulls me up.

I look down to make sure my dress has righted itself around my legs, which it has, and when I look back up, Nash's eyes aren't on my face; they're on my chest. I look down to see what he's staring at. Much to my embarrassment, all our . . . aggressive kissing caused my dress to shift a little. My boobs are practically spilling out. There's no Nipplegate or true wardrobe malfunction, but there is one hellacious amount of cleavage showing.

Nash is still holding my hand. I shake it loose and straighten my bodice. I can't help but grin at him when he finally meets my eyes.

"So that's how you charm the cobra," I quip.

He smiles devilishly. "If you really want to see what effect you have on my snake, I'd be happy to show you."

I feel blood rush to my cheeks and heat gush into my belly. Just like that, we're almost back where we started.

We stare at each other for several seconds and then Nash sighs. "I guess I should apologize again. I really don't act like this with most females. I swear."

Casually, he takes my hand again and leads me to the elevator.

"Not only am I glad to hear that, but I believe you," I assure him. And I do. Believe him, that is. He's a good guy. I can tell.

"You do?" he asks. By his expression, it seems like he actually *cares* what I think.

Huh! Go figure!

"Yeah, I do. I know the kind of guy you are."

"And what kind is that?" He ushers me onto the elevator.

"Smart, successful, driven, honorable."

He laughs. "Wow! Although flattering, that makes it sound like I should be either carrying a sword or meeting someone at dawn for a duel."

"I didn't mean it like that. I mean, you're all sorts of other things, but mostly you're a good guy. I can tell."

"And that's a good thing?" he asks, his expression dubious.

I smile. "To me, that's a very good thing."

He returns my smile and I have to look away. I feel like I've said too much. And I shouldn't have qualified my statement like I did.

Idiot.

"Well, as long as *you* think so . . ."

We fall into silence on the way to the parking garage. I can't think past the flurry of my emotions and the feel of his thumb stroking the back of my hand. I know we shouldn't be holding hands as though we're on a date, but I can't bring myself to pull my fingers free. This will be over all too soon; I'm going to enjoy every last second of it while I can. Tomorrow, reality returns. And, with it, Marissa.

Nash sticks with polite chitchat on the way back, which is fine. I don't have to think too much to participate. I can just . . . be. And bask. And fantasize.

I can easily imagine what it would be like to be heading home from a date with Nash. A real date. If he were mine. To have such a dashing, successful man at my side, one who turns me to mush with a look and sets me on fire with a touch. Nash is like the best of both worlds. But unfortunately, he belongs to a world I don't fit into.

But Marissa does.

"So how do you like working for my brother?"

Cash.

Just the thought of him, of his name, causes my stomach to twitch with excitement. The look he gave me as he bent his head to take the lime slice from between my lips was nothing short of predatory. Spending virtually any amount of time with a guy like that would be the ride of a lifetime. But then he'd leave me brokenhearted.

They always do.

"I gather by your silence that it didn't go well. Do I need to extend my apologies on my brother's behalf, too?"

I'm ashamed of myself for thinking of Cash when his equally gorgeous, equally hot twin is sitting in the seat beside me. And he was just kissing me in ways that Cash didn't, yet I *still* think of Cash and get all gooey.

Ohmigod, you are a head case! A whore *and a head case!*

"Olivia?"

I jerk back to the present. "Oh God, no! It went fine. I'm so sorry. I was thinking about work, actually. I have a shift on Wednesday."

"So you're enjoying it? And he was . . . all right to work with?"

There's something about his tone . . .

"Why do you ask? Did you expect that he might not be?"

Nash shrugs. "No. Not really."

"Not really?"

"Well . . ."

"Well what?"

"Cash is sort of a . . . a . . ."

"If it's got someone as eloquent as you at a loss for words, I can only imagine what it says about him."

"No, it's not like that. It's just that I figured Cash would like you."

"Well, I'm glad he did. It's going to save me a lot of time and gas money."

Nash tosses me a look of exasperation. "That's not what I meant, and you know it."

"What did you mean, then?"

"Olivia, you're beautiful, smart, funny. Any man would want you. And my brother is no different. He's just a little more . . . aggressive about what he wants. I didn't want him to run you off."

I think back to my banter with Cash about sexual harassment. I don't doubt he pushes the boundaries, but never once did I get the impression he might force himself on me or make unwanted advances. I just hope to God he doesn't know that his advances *aren't* unwanted. I wish they were.

"Well, you don't need to worry about Cash. He was a perfect gentleman and I have no reason to believe that might change. I work for him. He'll respect that."

From the corner of my eye, I see Nash look at me like I'm crazy. I ignore him.

Our conversation is cut short when we pull into the lot outside the townhouse I share with Marissa. I feel a sigh lurking in my chest. I know Nash won't come in. Because I won't ask him. And that's for the best.

It just happens to suck.

As I suspect, he puts the car in park but leaves the motor running.

It's for the best. It's for the best.

"Thank you," I say, meeting his dark, fathomless eyes. They look like points of onyx in the glow of the dashboard lights. "I had a really good time."

His laugh is a disbelieving bark. "No, you didn't."

I smile. "Okay, I had *mostly* a really good time. Thank you for bringing me. And I really hope—"

"Ah, ah, ah," he begins, cutting me off. "Not another word. None of what happened was your fault. I should've expected nothing less from a bunch of vapid trophy wives. Not your fault at all."

I can't help but think it's funny he uses two of the same adjectives I used for them earlier. Great minds . . .

"Well, the night would've turned out much differently if Marissa had been able to go with you. She'd have known exactly what to wear and . . ." I trail off, for the first time realizing that I've been sabotaged. There is no doubt in my mind that Marissa knew *exactly* what would happen if I turned up dressed like I am.

"And what?" Nash prompts.

I look over at him. He deserves so much better. So much more. I just wish I could give it to him. But I'd be career suicide for a guy like him.

"Oh, uh, just that she's much better suited to that kind of thing, that kind of crowd. I'm just a country girl."

Nash leans forward and cups my cheek with his hand. He cocks his head slightly as he considers me. "Don't do that. Don't ever make it out like you're less. Because you'd be gravely mistaken."

He looks straight into my eyes, as though he wants me to see the truth of his words, as if he wants me to see his sincerity. And I do. It's there. It just doesn't change anything. It doesn't change that he's with Marissa.

He's not that kind of guy. And I'm not that kind of girl.

"I appreciate that, Nash." I know I need to go. No matter how much I want him to kiss me again, no matter how much I want him to come to my room with me and finish what we started, I know I can't. I shouldn't. I won't. And neither will he.

But if he did . . .

I speak right over the top of that thought. There's no point in going there, because he won't.

"Good night, Nash."

His lips twist into a wry smile. I wonder what he was expecting. "Good night, beautiful Olivia."

Walking away from the car, away from Nash when there might be some small chance he would come with me, is the hardest thing I've ever done.

It's not until the next morning I even remember Nash told me his father was in prison for murder. That's pretty bad when my hormones can block out a homicide.

SIXTEEN

Cash

I've never really found it hard to stay away from a chick before. Hell, I've never had reason to try. But this time I do. There's something different about Olivia. I want her in my bed. Like, now. But she's . . . I don't know. I get the feeling she requires a gentler, more careful touch. She's a challenge.

And damn, if I don't love a challenge!

I watch her as she pours a drink with Taryn looking over her shoulder. I could pull Taryn to the side and demand that she ease up on Olivia, but I won't. Not only do I think it's good for Olivia—it brings out that feisty side of her—but I think she'd rather handle it herself. And I admire that. A lot. The more I'm around her, the more obvious it becomes that there's a lot more to her than a shy smile and a pretty face.

And, of course, a body that I can't wait to get inside.

And I will.

And she'll enjoy every second of it. I'll make sure of it.

SEVENTEEN

Olivia

It seems like every time I look up, I see Cash. Sometimes he's talking to customers, doing his owner-slash-manager thing. But other times, often it seems, he's watching me. It makes me nervous, but not in a performance-anxiety kind of way. I'm confident in my ability to make a good drink, even with a drill sergeant squawking in my ear. What I'm *not* confident in is my ability to resist what Cash isn't even trying to hide.

He's interested in me. And not just as an employee. Maybe very little as an employee, in fact. Every time my eyes meet his, I feel like he's undressing me. And, God help me, I love it. Those sexy, velvety eyes are like a touch. I can almost feel them, like hands on my body and lips on my mouth.

Admittedly, I have a thing for bad boys, but Cash is . . . I don't know. He's different. I daresay he's even *more* dangerous than my usual disastrous finds.

I look up and my eyes collide with his again. He winks at me and my stomach flips over.

"That's not how we make margaritas here," Taryn snaps in my ear. "Who uses orange juice?"

I exhale so loudly it sounds like a growl. I could explain how a splash of orange juice adds a little something extra to the flavor of the tequila, but I don't. I've had enough of Taryn's bitchiness. "Fine," I say, setting down the tequila bottle a little more forcefully than I intended. "Then show me how you make margaritas here." I stand back and cross my arms over my chest.

The look Taryn throws me is both angry and satisfied. Obviously, she wanted me to crack. Well, she's about to get more than she bargained for.

"Well, get on it. Show me. People are waiting," I say in my calmest voice, tipping my head to indicate the cluster of people surrounding us on the other side of the bar.

Her pale blue eyes flash with anger and her ruby red lips tighten. She's ready for a fight. And so am I.

"You'd better leave that attitude at the door, honey, or tonight's likely to be your last."

I hear the hushed voices go up all around us—*oooh*s and *aaah*s and whispers of a catfight. I ignore them and focus on Taryn.

"Is that right? You think you've got the pull to get rid of me just because you're a compulsive control freak with an obsessive need for attention?"

Taryn's laugh is bitter, but she doesn't bother to deny it. I think she knows I'm right.

It hadn't taken me long to peg her for what she is—an insecure girl with daddy issues. After my body-shot audition, she had gone above and beyond to draw every eye away from me and down the bar to her. She'd changed the music to an upbeat song by Jessie James and proceeded to dance along the bar, lip-synching "Wanted" to every male within viewing distance.

And, of course, they loved it. I mean, she's gorgeous, even with long blond dreads, and she's sexy in a very feline kind of way. What guy with a functioning penis wouldn't love a girl like that up on display, teasing him mercilessly?

But I knew it was more for my benefit than anything else. As she was climbing down off the bar, she gave me a smug little smile. She was showing me up, showing me that she *could* show me up. What she doesn't understand is that I don't want all the attention. She's welcome to it.

Thinking of it this way cools my temper considerably. I decide to give her what she wants—the love of all the men.

"What do you say to a little contest? Loser has to do a bar dance."

I'm a little surprised at her hesitation, but then when I see her eyes flicker to my right, I understand what her problem is. Cash is mingling with a group of gushing girls not far from where we are.

Then I get it. I really get it.

Holy shit! She's got a thing for Cash!

My first thought is that I don't blame her. I think everything with estrogen likes Cash. My second thought is wonderment that they haven't already slept together. That's not very bad-boy-like of him.

Unless they have and she's just not over it. That would be much more bad-boy-like.

For some reason, jealousy gnaws at my insides.

"You're on," she says with a nod.

"Best margarita wins. Both are on me," I say, then turn to the handful of guys watching and listening to us. "Who wants to judge?"

Of course, they all start clamoring to be chosen. But it's not an issue when Cash steps in.

"I'll be the judge," he offers, his eyes daring me in the low light of the bar. "I think it's only fair."

"Of course," I say, feeling a bit breathless when he's so close and I'm in his sights. I look to Taryn. Her look has gone from hostile to downright murderous. It occurs to me that what began as a solid plan could very well backfire. "That okay with you?"

"Fine by me," she says, turning a brilliant smile on Cash. "I know what he likes."

The guys around the bar start hollering and whistling at that, nudging and teasing Cash. Cash just smiles at Taryn. And it bugs me. I can't tell whether there's something between them or not. Or if it's just a tolerant employer-type smile.

I hope if there ever was *anything between them that it's over.*

It chaps my butt to think of him flirting like he does with

me, watching me, teasing me, all the while sleeping with Taryn. It shouldn't matter. He's a playboy and that's what playboys do.

But it does matter.

Dammit!

"Come on, boys. Let's give 'em a little help," Cash says. The people around him start cheering enthusiastically. Cash smiles at them and then turns to face me, leaning forward a little on the bar. His eyes meet mine and one brow rises in that *holy mother of hell* sexy way, then he mutters, "You've got one chance to make my mouth water."

I suck in a breath. And chills break out down my arms.

Damn, he's good!

I'm so glad for the room full of people. Otherwise, I might embarrass myself by stripping off all my clothes and climbing across the bar to wind all my body parts around him.

Caution is nowhere in my head when I taunt him in return. "Oh, I can do better than that."

His lips curve into a nerve-racking smile. "I don't doubt that one bit."

Dragging my eyes and my attention away from him, I put all my concentration into making a good drink. It's much more difficult than it should be. My eyes keep trying to stray to Cash.

As I'm rubbing the rim of the glass in salt, I forget and look up. Cash is singing along to a song about whistling and when the part comes for him to whistle, he puckers up his perfect mouth and does it right along with the beat.

I can't help but stare. And, as if he doesn't already have me flustered enough, when he stops whistling, my eyes climb back to his and he winks at me.

It's the exact moment I know I'm in trouble. Big, big trouble.

Taryn pushes me to the side to slide a glass across the bar in front of Cash. It pulls me from my thrall. I pour my margarita, garnish it with a wedge of lime and a wedge of orange, and offer it up as well.

He sips first Taryn's drink then mine and then each one again, smacking his lips and savoring the flavors. I wonder if he'll really pick the best drink, or if he'll simply pick the one *opposite* the girl he'd rather see dance on the bar.

I realize there isn't an outcome I'll be happy with. If he chooses my drink as the best, I'll wonder if it's because he wants to see Taryn dance. Not that it should matter to me what he wants to see Taryn do.

But it does.

Dammit.

But then, if he chooses her drink, not only will her drink be supposedly better, but I'll have to dance on the bar, which I really don't want to do.

He nods and picks up my drink to finish it off. "We have a winner!" he says, pointing to me.

I feel relieved and victorious, but also strangely conflicted. Rather than look him in the eye, I remove the empty glass when Cash sets it down on the bar. My eyes move past Taryn, who is smiling coyly at someone, I assume Cash.

"Good news, boys," she yells happily. "I'm still gonna be

making margaritas *my* way, *and* you'll be getting some entertainment tonight. I call that a win-win."

With a whoop, Taryn reaches back to flip on different music, choosing a very suggestive song that I have no doubt she'll make good use of. When I see her climb up on the bar, I move to the opposite end to get drinks for the handful of people who aren't watching her and cheering her on.

I do everything I can not to watch her *or* Cash. I don't want to see his reaction. But when the cheers get louder, my eyes are drawn down the bar despite my resolve.

Taryn apparently jumped off the bar into Cash's arms. He's cradling her and she has her arms wrapped around his neck, very tightly, it appears. She's smiling like the cat who ate the canary—or maybe the cat who *wants* to eat the canary—and Cash is laughing.

Just as I'm looking back to the draft I'm pouring, I see Taryn pull Cash's head down to hers and kiss him. And it's not just a little peck. She looks like she's trying to swallow his face. And he's not resisting.

Cold liquid gushing over my fingers pulls me back to the task at hand. The pilsner is overflowing and beer is running down my wrist and into the spill tray. I jerk back and set the glass down, angrily flinging beer from my fingertips. I'm inordinately mad at myself for letting Taryn and Cash rile me up, and even more so for letting it affect me so blatantly.

I'm making furious swipes over the wet counter, cleaning up my mess, when Cash leans across the bar and speaks to me.

"I need you to stay after for just a few minutes tonight. Got some paperwork for you to fill out. Shouldn't take long."

I look up and meet his eyes. I want to scratch them out. And then spit in his face. And then curse him for being exactly what I thought he was.

A bad boy.

A playboy.

A heartbreaker.

But I also want to kiss him. And let him carry me up to the private room above us and put an end to the dull ache of desire that's been plaguing me since the first night we met when I pulled his shirt over his head.

Dammit!

He smiles as he leans back. "Great drink, by the way." He slaps the bar twice, like a pat on the back, and walks off toward the mysterious door at the back of the room.

That's officially the point where my night takes a nosedive.

Strangely, what I'd thought would help Taryn's disposition seems only to have made her more hostile. Unfortunately for her, my mood has plummeted, taking my patience and tolerance with it. So for the rest of the night, I give just as good as I get.

Even though I dread having to talk to Cash, I'm really relieved when the night is over. Taryn and I had graduated from thinly veiled remarks to her shoulder-bumping me as she passed, to me purposely backing into her while she was pouring a round of lemon drop shooters. From there, it escalated to her pushing a drink into the floor and splashing Bailey's all up my legs. It made a horrendous sticky mess that took me far too long to clean up. At that point, I figured the only logical progression would be hair pulling and vicious clawing as we roll around in the floor, growling at each other. And, call me crazy, but I'm thinking that kind of thing might be frowned upon in all places of business that *do not* include a Jell-O pit.

That's when I stopped antagonizing her. Now, I'm just ready to go home.

As I'm closing up my end of the bar, I'm thankful I remember most of what Marco showed me. The things I'm a little fuzzy on I'm able to improvise by sneaking peeks down at what Taryn's doing on her end. She's just faster at it than I am. Obviously.

When she's finished cleaning up her area, she practically runs around the bar and makes for the door at the back of the room. She doesn't even glance in my direction, much less say anything to me. And I couldn't care less, really. Her attitude isn't the reason my stomach is in knots. My stomach is in knots because I think I have a very good idea of who's doing whom tonight.

For that reason, I take my sweet time cleaning up. I'd rather die than interrupt them. In fact, I really wish he'd just forget about my paperwork and let me go home.

I'm berating myself for giving a guy like Cash a second thought when Taryn comes out of the room. I look up. At first glance, she seems . . . bothered. But when she sees me looking at her, she turns on her brightest smile, grabs her purse from behind the bar, and walks merrily out the front door.

I want to paper-cut her. On every square inch of her body. And then roll her in saltwater.

Just the thought of that has me snickering to myself, which is what I'm doing when Cash comes out. He's not adjusting his clothes or anything that obvious, but I know what he's been up to. And I'm furious.

"You about done?" he asks casually.

I snort. "Are you?" I could kick myself for letting my upset show, but it sort of slips out before I can stop it.

Cash's brow wrinkles for just a second. "I'm ready whenever you are. I know you need to get home."

How convenient that you remember that now! *You're probably ready for bed. A real* bed.

Gritting my teeth, I toss my rag into the bleach and snatch my purse from beneath the bar. I refuse to rush just because he's finally ready. Refuse! Yes, I'll be the one paying for it when I'm exhausted tomorrow, but tonight passive-aggressive is all I've got.

He leads the way back to the carefully concealed door at the back of the bar. As I suspected, it's an office. And a nicely decorated office, too. Especially considering that it's located in a bar.

The color palette is both soothing and masculine with its rich creams and calming taupes. There are black accents found throughout the room in the throw pillows on the sofa and the lamps on the end tables. They tie in to the huge black desk and expertly carved cabinetry behind it.

There's a partially open door on the back wall. It looks as

though it leads into an apartment. A very nice and spacious one, from what I can see.

With a sinking sensation, I realize he and Taryn were probably back there. In a real bed.

I feel sick.

Cash motions me to a plush black-and-taupe striped chair in front of the desk as he takes the black leather chair behind it. He clicks a few buttons on the computer and prints off some forms, sliding them across the desk to me. I take a pen from the cup of pens sitting to my left.

Silently, I fill out the necessary tax forms and employee forms as Cash makes what I assume is an employee file. When I'm finished and there are no more papers to sign, I lay down my pen and wait. He finally looks up at me and smiles.

"So, how are you liking it? Besides Taryn, of course."

I force my lips into a smile. "Fine, thank you."

I see a frown flicker across his forehead again. "Is there anything you need to talk about? Anything I can do to make your job easier?"

Other than stay the hell away from me?

I bite my tongue and hold my smile in place, shaking my head negatively. He nods, watching me closely. "All right; well, I guess I'd better let you get on home, then."

With a curt nod, I stand and leave as quickly as I can without being obvious. After I've passed through the exit and am making my way to the brightly lit parking lot, I give in to the urge to scream in angry frustration. Just a little. It's more like a growl, actually.

I stomp to my car, throwing my purse onto the hood to search inside for the keys. That's when I hear footsteps. I whirl, startled, as Cash comes to a stop beside me.

"Are you all right?"

His frown is still in place, but his eyes are wide. He's obviously concerned. He probably heard my scream-growl, since he was coming outside.

Great!

"I'm fine," I hiss. "Go back inside. I'm just leaving."

"I forgot to give you your copy of the release of liability," he explains, handing me a folded sheet of paper.

I snatch it from his fingers and stuff it into my purse. "Thank you. Good night," I say dismissively, returning my attention to the hunt for my keys.

Cash grabs my shoulders and turns me toward him. "What is your deal?"

And I snap.

"Get your hands off me," I demand, wrenching away from him. He looks stricken, which only makes me madder. "You don't get to touch me. I'm not Taryn."

"What?" He looks genuinely confused. Then he rolls his eyes. And I see red. "Is this about that kiss?"

I ball my hands into fists. It's all I can do not to physically lash out at him. "No, it's not just about the kiss. It's about kisses and body shots and late-night booty calls in your office and an assortment of things that shouldn't be going on here!"

I'm getting loud and I know it. I've also taken a step forward that puts me right up next to Cash's chest, which is where my index finger is currently buried. I look at it as if I have no idea how it got there, mainly because I don't.

I look up at Cash, but he's looking at my finger, too. Slowly, deliberately, he wraps his long fingers around my hand, then straightens his arm, pulling it out to his side. He tugs sharply, nearly causing me to fall into him.

"Is that what this is about? You think I'm sleeping with Taryn?"

"Of course I do! I'm sure it's no secret."

"Why do you say that?"

He's so calm. Curious almost. It's disconcerting.

"Well, first of all, she's gorgeous and—"

"You're gorgeous," he says softly.

My stomach flips over, but I continue. "And she flirts very openly with you."

"I wish you would flirt very openly with me." His eyes flicker to my lips, and they throb like he's touching them.

"Stop doing that. Don't act like there's nothing going on."

"I'm not acting. Taryn and I have a history, but that was before she started working for me. I have few rules, but one is that I don't get social with my employees. And now she works for me. That's it. Nothing more."

"But you kissed her. I saw you."

"No, you saw *her* kiss *me*. You saw *me* not cause a scene in the middle of the club."

"Well, you didn't look like you hated it."

"But I did. The whole time, all I could think about was kissing you instead." He starts to bend his head toward mine.

Blood is roaring in my ears. "But you don't get social with your employees," I remind him quietly.

"I'd make an exception for you." His face is getting close and closer. Slowly. A centimeter at a time.

"But it's your rule."

"I'll break it for you," he whispers.

"No, don't do that," I say breathlessly.

"Fine, then you're fired," he says just as his lips meet mine.

They are warm and the pressure is light. At first. As much as I want to resist, my resolve goes out the window when I feel his tongue run along the crease of my lips. Without thinking, I part them.

And that's all it takes.

The taste of Cash is like a perfectly aged Scotch—rich and delicious. His tongue slides along mine, stroking it, teasing it, as he uses his grip on my hand to pull me tighter to him. I do the only thing I can. I melt into him.

The fingers of his free hand work their way into my hair and tilt my head to the side as he deepens the kiss. He gets more aggressive, like he wants to gobble me up. And I want him to. God, I want him to.

He releases my hand and I feel his palm at the base of my spine. He splays his fingers and presses me into him.

He's hard. And he's huge. I can feel him against my belly. Warmth gushes through me, pooling between my legs. It's been so long and I know instinctively that any sexual time spent with Cash would be an earth-shattering, soul-screaming, body-rocking time.

Time that I'd probably live to regret when I got too close and he got too bored.

The reality of what I'm doing slaps me in the face and I pull back. My hands are in his hair, my body is glued to his, and I ache for him from head to toe. But still, I pull back.

"What's the matter?" he asks, his eyes dark with passion and peppered with confusion.

"We can't do this."

"I was just kidding about firing you."

"That's not what I mean."

"Then what *do* you mean?"

He steps back to give me room, but he grabs my hands to keep me from completely retreating. I don't know why I let him hold them. Probably because I really don't want him to let go. I just know that I *should*.

"Cash, all my life I've picked the wrong guy. The bad boy, the wild child, the rebel without a cause. I bet you didn't even graduate high school, did you?" Cash doesn't correct me, doesn't deny it. "See? That's the kind of guy I'm attracted to. *You're* the kind of guy I'm attracted to. I won't even pretend I'm not. But you're the worst thing in the world for me. I've had my heart broken one too many times, and I'm done. I'm done trying to tame the guys like you."

He watches me closely, nodding slowly. "I understand that. I really do. But you want me and I want you. Can't we just have that?"

My mouth drops open a little. "You're kidding, right?"

"No."

"You're seriously asking to have meaningless sex with me?"

"Oh, it won't be meaningless," he declares with a grin. "It will be everything you want it to be, with the understanding that, in the end, we'll go our separate ways."

"That's the problem. Who picks when the end will be? You?"

"No, you can decide that. Or we can decide that together. Up front. We can stop when you're ready to stop. Or before it becomes something you don't want it to become."

I know I should be offended, not intrigued. "But that's just . . . just . . ."

"It's just like the majority of other relationships without all the lies and expectations. That's all it is. It's practical and it's smart."

"A practical, smart sexual relationship?" I know my look is dubious. It has to be.

"Yes, but also a fiery, exciting, intensely pleasurable one," he says, his voice dropping into a slower, deeper cadence. He steps toward me again. "I promise you won't regret it. I promise to make you feel things and enjoy things you never even thought of before. I'll make every night the best night of your life until you say it's over. And then I'll walk away. No hard feelings. Only sweet, sweet memories," he purrs as he rubs our joined hands up and down the outsides of his thighs.

I know I should be slapping him or laughing in his face or at least pretending to be deeply insulted, which I should be. Yet I'm not. Instead, I'm actually considering what he's saying.

Cash is smart enough to know when to pull back and let things ride. So he does.

"Give it some thought. We can talk more this weekend. In the meantime," he whispers as he bends near my ear, "think about how it will feel to have my tongue inside you." He nips my lobe with his teeth, and I feel it all the way in the pit of my stomach. I bite my lip to keep from moaning. "And I'll be thinking about what you taste like."

And then, damn him, he turns around and walks off, leaving me standing in a puddle near the hood of my car.

EIGHTEEN

Nash

I've stayed away from Marissa on purpose, just so I don't run into Olivia. Not only could she screw up my plans in a big way, she doesn't deserve all the trouble I come with. She didn't seem too concerned when I told her about Dad, but that's just the tip of the iceberg. Well, maybe not the tip, but it's still just a small portion of the mess in my life.

But, as usual, Marissa started getting pouty and demanding, so here I am, soothing ruffled feathers over coffee. I glance at my watch. I'm really hoping to miss Olivia altogether. I think I remember Marissa saying she has her early classes on Mondays and Wednesdays. I need to be gone before she gets up. Seeing her will only make it harder to stay away from her. A man can only be pushed so far before he gives in, regardless of the consequences.

"If it weren't important, I'm sure he wouldn't be asking me to go," Marissa is saying. I'm sure it's something I should be paying attention to, not ignoring while I think about her cousin.

"I'm sorry, go where?"

She sticks out her lip. "What's wrong with you? I wanted you to come over so I could spend some time with you before I left, not talk to you while you stare into your coffee."

I sigh. "I'm sorry, babe. I just keep thinking about that case Carl has me working on." I set my mug down and reach for her hands. Her ice-cold hands.

Damn, that's fitting.

"Tell me again. I'm all yours," I declare with a smile.

"Daddy wants me to go with two of the senior staff to Grand Cayman to look over those accounts. I'm hoping that means he's gonna let me in on the whole project."

I understand her excitement. I'm envious of the opportunity. She's three years older than me, so she's already graduated and practicing law, while I'm still stuck in internship for another few months.

"That's great! I'm so proud of you. I'll miss you, of course, but when do you leave?"

"Tomorrow." She's still pouting.

"And how long will you be gone?"

"At least two weeks. Could be longer."

"Well, that just gives us good reason to celebrate when you get back, because I'll have missed you *and* you'll have good news. I'm sure of it." I pull her to me and she plops down on my lap. She winds her thin arms around my neck and kisses me. I know all I'd have to do is pick her up and carry her into the bedroom and I could have an early-morning quickie, but I don't. I'm not that heartless and inconsiderate, because even as she's in my lap, wiggling around and kissing me, I'm thinking of bright green eyes, jet-black hair, and the luscious little body sleeping just a couple rooms away. And that's not cool.

Marissa leans back and frowns down at me. "You still seem distracted."

"I'm fine. Really. I just need to get going. I was supposed to be getting some paperwork ready over an hour ago."

She smiles. "So you're saying you're blowing off work to spend the morning with me?"

"Yep. That's what I'm saying."

She gets that look in her eyes and she presses her upper body into mine and rubs back and forth. Obligingly, I cup her small breasts and stroke her hard nipples with my thumbs. Her lids close a little and I know where this is going.

And then a throat clears. Both Marissa and I look up to see Olivia standing in the doorway, looking sleepy yet horrified.

"What?" Marissa snaps. "Get your coffee and go. We're a little busy."

She turns back to me to pick up where we left off, but I stop her. "I really need to go." Without giving her a chance to say much else, I scoot her off my lap and stand. From the corner of my eye, I can see Olivia looking at me. I avoid eye contact at all costs. I can feel her shooting daggers at my heart, though. And at my dick. I'm sure she's just about ready to spew venom and hatred all over the kitchen floor. What she doesn't know, though, is that I hate myself ten times more than she could ever hate me for what I did, for what almost happened.

"But wait. I wanted to ask you if you'd pick up my car from the shop on Monday. I'll leave my keys for you."

"Fine," I say hurriedly, grabbing her hand and towing her out of the kitchen.

If Olivia wanted me to feel guilty, mission accomplished!

"I'll call you later," I say, pecking her on the lips. "Maybe we can have dinner tonight." In my head, I'm thinking I'll say anything to get out of here.

"I can't! I'm going to spend the night with Mom and then we're riding to the airport together with Daddy in the morning. Hang on. Let me get you my keys. I can call for the limo later."

She rushes off, leaving me standing by the door waiting, hoping Olivia stays put. But she doesn't. Of course.

I see her come to stand in the doorway. Although it's against my better judgment, I turn to look at her. In her eyes is embarrassment and disappointment and shame, yes, but there's also the spark of whatever is between us. There's just no denying that we're attracted to each other. Very, very attracted to each other.

I hear Marissa's voice. She's on the phone with someone, so I move toward Olivia.

I don't really know what to say, so I just stand there, staring down at her. She really is breathtaking, even first thing in the morning.

Before I even realize what I'm doing, I rub my fingertips down her smooth cheek. Her eyelids flutter shut, making me want to kiss them.

"Sorry about that," I hear Marissa say as she comes down the hall. I step back and walk to the door, stopping where she left me. I glance quickly back at Olivia. There's a mixture of emotions on her face, emotions I can't easily identify. Unless it's the same thing I'm feeling, too.

NINETEEN

Olivia

Maybe it's PMS. Maybe it's just the stress of too much change too quickly. I have no idea really, but I feel like all of a sudden, my life is a train wreck.

And most of the wreckage revolves around two guys. Two guys who, for totally different reasons, are tearing me up inside. Two guys I want. Two guys I can't have. Two guys I can't stop thinking about.

I want Cash—badly—on a purely physical level, although he is cute and charming, which only adds to the danger level. But I want Nash just as badly, in a different way. There's a physical component for sure. He turns me on something fierce. But he's just the *kind of guy* that I want, that I *need* in my life.

I don't think I retained a single word from any of my three

classes today. I'm more thankful than ever that a lot of it is fluff stuff—statistics, sociology, and body mechanics, which is like the college version of gym class.

By the time I get back home, I'm exhausted. More emotionally than physically, but it ends up feeling like the same thing. In the quiet of the house, knowing I'll have it all to myself for two weeks (a fact which I gleaned accidentally rather than Marissa actually telling me herself), I decide to lie down on the couch to take a short nap.

I wake up at four thirty, feeling no better. Just dead-headed. I'm still feeling icky in general, so I reach for my phone and call Shawna. I get her voice mail, which informs me she's with her mom picking out flowers for the wedding.

The only other really close friend I have is Ginger, the bartender I worked with at Tad's for years. Thankfully, she's home.

After we talk for several minutes, she gets blunt, Ginger style. "All right, spill it. Something's wrong."

"No, nothing's wrong."

"You're a terrible liar and I hate you for trying."

I giggle. "No, you don't."

She pauses. "Okay, I don't. But the only way you can make it up to me is to tell me what the hell's up your butt."

Ginger also has a way with words.

I sigh. "I guess I'm just missing home and friends and . . . I don't know. Life just feels . . . complicated."

"Uh-huh. This sounds like penis problems."

"Ohmigod, Ginger! It's not penis problems. You think everything is about sex."

"Isn't it?"

I laugh. "No. It's not."

"So this has nothing to do with a guy?"

I pause.

"Aha! I knew it! Penis problems."

"Well, it seems that the *cause* of some of my problems happens to *have* a penis. Well, two actually."

"Oh, sweet Mary! You're dating a guy with two dicks?"

"Ginger, no! It's about two different guys."

"Oh," she says, obviously disappointed. "Damn. That woulda been kinda cool."

"How so?"

"I don't know. One for each hole?"

"You're sick, you know that?"

"Yeah, pretty much."

I laugh again. "At least you're not afraid to admit it."

"Girl, I own it! I'm too old to pretend to be something I'm not. Takes too much effort. Just like faking orgasms. If you don't bring your A-game, don't bother showing up at all. I've only got a limited number of orgasmic years left. I plan to squeeze every last drop of pleasure out of them that I can. And I *do mean squeeze.*"

I roll my eyes and shake my head. *Oh, Ginger . . .*

After a few more minutes of wildly inappropriate shock-and-awe talk, Ginger promises to come take me out for drinks tonight, which actually sounds like a lifeline. We make plans to meet at a pub she's familiar with downtown and, by the time we're hanging up, I'm already feeling more lighthearted.

I'm finishing my second drink when my cell phone rings. My heart sinks when I see Ginger's number.

"Where are you?" I ask without preamble.

"I can't make it tonight, sweetie. Tad needs some help. Norma called in sick and he needs the help. I just turned around to head back home. I'm so sorry, Liv. I'll make it up to you. I promise."

I grit my teeth. "That's fine, Ginger. We'll do it another time."

"In the meantime, get those penis problems fixed. Every henhouse needs a cock, but only the special hens can handle more than one. Try 'em out, then pick one and stick with it. You're not old enough to play with two toys at the same time. That's cougar territory."

"I'll try to remember that," I say derisively.

"You just send the rejected one my way. I'll make him forget all about you. At least for a few hours." She laughs in her gravelly smoker's voice. "Talk soon, sweetie. Smooches." And then she's gone.

I hang up and look around the bar. As much as I really don't want to go back to an empty house and think about all my troubles, I don't really want to stay here by myself, either. With a depressed sigh, I slide a few dollars under my empty glass and scoot off the bar stool, digging my keys out of my purse as I go.

Try 'em out, then pick one and stick with it.

Ginger's words run through my head. They sound ludicrous! And completely slutty. But at the same time . . .

No matter how much I want it to work, the thing with Nash is impossible. He's dating Marissa. I mean, I saw them together this morning. Even now it makes me sick to think about it.

But then I remember him brushing my face. It makes me wonder if I'm in his head like he's in mine.

And then there's Cash. At least a relationship with him would be less complicated. Less meaningful, with less of a future, of course, but at least I'd know what's what.

Insane thoughts are running through my head as I get in and start the car. Or should I say *try to start* the car.

What now?

I bang my hand on the steering wheel as the lights flicker weakly. "No, no, no!"

I turn on the interior light and it barely sheds a dim cone of illumination into the backseat. These are sick-car symptoms I'm familiar with, ones I know.

The battery.

"You are such a piece of shit," I yell into the quiet cab, slapping the horn accidentally. It makes a sound like a wounded duck. "Don't you talk back to me! You're this close to going to car heaven at the junkyard."

Yes, it makes me feel a tiny bit better to get rid of some of my frustration, even if it means sitting outside a pub, yelling at an inanimate object. A very inanimate at the moment.

Now what?

I need someone to jump me. I hate to call a tow truck for

something so simple. It would cost me a fortune. And my friend resource pool is frighteningly shallow here.

That's what happens when you spend the first two years up a guy's ass and the third one as a wallflower.

I close my eyes and try to think. As always, two faces, identical faces, float through my mind.

Nash probably has plans. According to Marissa, he stays incredibly busy. I'd hate to play the damsel-in-distress card and interrupt him, no matter how much I like the thought of him coming to save me.

Then I think of Cash. He owns his own business and disappears for hours at a time pretty regularly each night. Plus he's just a few blocks away. He would be the logical choice. But remembering our last conversation, my stomach flutters with nerves wondering what he might ask for in the form of payment.

I can't deny that the prospect excites me, though.

Try 'em out.

Pushing Ginger's voice out of my head, I reach for my cell phone and pick out Cash's number from the contact list. He answers on the second ring.

"Cash, this is Olivia."

"What's up?" he says abruptly. His clipped tone surprises me. I don't know what I expected, but this isn't it. Maybe I thought he'd be all schmoozy and sexy, and try to talk me into sleeping with him. The sad thing is, I'm a little disappointed that he's not.

"Am I bothering you? Because I can totally—"

"You're not bothering me. What's up?" he repeats.

"Well, I hate to call you over something like this, but my car battery is dead, I think, and I'm sort of stuck. I was wondering if you could come and jump me. I'm just a few blocks away."

There's a pause. And it feels like a long pause, especially when I'm already on pins and needles. I think for a second of just hanging up. How childish would that be? Yeah, after doing something that embarrassing, I'd be forced to quit Dual, quit school, move back home, and leave all my recent humiliation behind in the big city. And as drastic as that sounds, sometimes it seems incredibly appealing.

But I don't. I just wait. While my face burns in humiliation.

"Tell me where you are."

I give him the address.

"Will you be all right for about fifteen minutes? There's just something I have to do before I can leave, but then I'll be right there."

"That's fine. Take your time."

"Can you go back inside and have a drink while you wait? I don't like the idea of you sitting outside in your car by yourself. You *are* by yourself, aren't you?"

"Yes, I'm alone. But I'll be fine. I just—"

"Olivia, I really don't like it. Can't you just go back inside? Consider it a favor."

When he puts it like that . . . "Okay. I'll go back inside. Just call me when you get here."

"See you in a few," he says, then hangs up.

Tossing my phone in my purse, I pull down the visor and

check my makeup. I know I shouldn't care, but I'm glad I got all dolled up to meet Ginger. After I reapply a little rose lipstick, I run my fingers through my straight hair and adjust my red off-the-shoulder shirt.

Back inside, I order a beer. It's inexpensive, so I don't mind leaving it when Cash shows up, plus sipping it won't give me a buzz.

Twenty minutes pass and I've checked my phone for the sixth time. I'm beginning to wonder if everyone's going to stand me up tonight when the door swings open and I look up to see Cash striding toward me.

My mouth goes completely dry when his eyes meet mine and he smiles a lopsided, cocky grin. I wish his long legs didn't devour the space between us so quickly. I could just look at him, just watch him move all day long. He's built so perfectly and he looks stunningly edible in his "work clothes" of snug black jeans, a snug black T-shirt, and black boots. It sets off his wide shoulders, his narrow waist, and the honey color of his skin. And those eyes. Damn those black eyes. They sparkle like drops of an ebony pond in his handsome face.

By the time he gets to me, I'm debating the need for a change of panties.

I start to slide off my stool, but he stops me. "Finish your beer," he says, then nods to the bartender. "Jack. Neat."

When the bartender slides his drink across to him, Cash takes a sip, then turns to me, as if he's settling in. "So, why are you here, drinking all by yourself tonight?"

Nervously, I use my thumbnail to scrape at the label on my

beer bottle. "I was supposed to be meeting someone, but they had to cancel. After I'd already gotten here, of course," I explain, bitterness dripping from my voice.

"Want me to kick his ass?" he asks. I look up at him, and he's grinning at me over the top of his glass.

"No. You might be embarrassed when *she* gets the better of you."

"Ahhhh, your butch girlfriend?"

His eyes are twinkling. He's teasing me. And enjoying himself tremendously, apparently. This is more like what I was expecting when I called. Well, not even this much, really. This playfulness is unexpected and very . . . disarming.

Don't let him charm you.

But then I think of Ginger's words again. And I get a little bolder.

"No, I'm not into girls. I very much like . . . men."

I can't help but wonder if the *vampy* in my head comes across as *campy* instead.

Too late.

"I got the feeling you might be last night."

He arches that one brow and his lips twitch with the smile he's containing.

Holy shit! He's so effing sexy.

"What's that supposed to mean?"

"It's kinda hard to describe," he says, leaning toward me and lowering his voice. "But I'd be happy to show you if you like."

There's a dare in his eyes. But I just don't know if I'm up

for all that he's offering. Can I go there without letting my heart get involved?

I clear my throat and look back at my beer bottle, backing down simply out of a need for self-preservation.

Smart guy that he is, he picks up on the shift in my mood.

"So," he says in a very nonchalant manner, "tell me all about Olivia."

I shrug. "There's not much to tell. I'm from Salt Springs. I grew up on my father's sheep farm and I'm a senior in college."

"Wow, a lifetime reduced to two sentences. I'm not sure if I'm *im*pressed or *de*pressed. Were there boyfriends and parties mixed in there? Or . . ."

I smile. "Yeah, there were a few of each. I wasn't a wild child, but I wasn't a shut-in, either. Just average, I guess."

"There's nothing average about you," Cash says quietly.

My eyes fly to his. He's not smiling and he doesn't appear to be teasing me, which triggers my blush.

"Thank you."

We stare at each other for a few seconds, right up until the air starts crackling with electricity between us. That's when I look away.

"So what's your major?"

"Accounting."

"Accounting? Accounting is for spinsters who wear their hair in a bun and have a closet full of orthopedic shoes. Why'd you pick accounting?"

I laugh at his vision. "I'm good with numbers. Plus, with

an accounting degree I'll be able to help Dad with the business. It just makes sense."

"So you're doing it for your dad?"

"Partly."

He nods slowly. The expression on his face says he doesn't believe me, but he says nothing. He just changes the subject.

"What about Mom?"

"She left. A long time ago."

His eyes narrow on me, but again he says nothing. He's a very perceptive guy.

"And this bad-boy boyfriend?"

"Bad boy?"

"Yeah. The type you apparently avoid now."

"Oh, right." I laugh. It's one single bark of bitterness. "Ummm, he fell into a wood chipper?" I ask, hoping he'll get the hint that I don't really want to talk about him, either.

He pauses with his drink halfway to his mouth, as if judging whether I'm serious, and then he grins and takes a sip.

"Poor guy. And the one before that?"

"Eaten by a shark?"

"And before that?"

"Kidnapped by a traveling circus?"

He chuckles. "Wow. Your life's like a cautionary tale."

"Future suitors be warned."

"I'm willing to take my chances," he says with a wink.

My stomach flutters in response and my heart does a funny flip that is, in and of itself, a huge red flag.

Change the subject! Change the subject!

"So, what about your family?"

That cools his teasing mood considerably. "A long, horrible story, too awful for the likes of your tender ears."

"Oh, is that so? So *you* can ask all kinds of questions, but this is all I get?"

I'm only half teasing. I really do want him to answer some questions, especially while I've got my wits about me. Somewhat, anyway.

"My questionable upbringing and suspicious connections might make you shake in your boots," he jokes with a not-quite-half smile.

I turn on my stool and look down at my feet. "I'm not wearing boots."

"I can see that," Cash says, reaching down to brush his palm up my calf. "No pantyhose, either."

A bubble of air is trapped in my throat, making it impossible for me to breathe. Chills break out and shoot up my leg, straight into my panties.

He looks up at me, his eyes flashing. I know what he wants. And I know he knows I want it, too. It's there in his eyes. There's no reason for me to even try to deny it. But what to do about it?

In my indecision, I turn my legs back toward the bar, away from his hand. He smiles. Knowingly. But he goes along.

For now.

He finishes his drink in one long pull, then turns to me. I push my beer away.

"You ready?"

Talk about your loaded question!

I nod. I'm not sure what all I just agreed to, but every nerve in my body is alive with anticipation.

"Come on," he says with a tip of his head and a wicked grin. "Let's go get you off."

I can't help but smile.

TWENTY

Cash

I can't keep my hands off Olivia as we leave the bar. Not completely, anyway. As she steps out in front of me, I put my hand at the base of her spine. I feel her twitch at the contact. It's not a flinch, but an actual twitch. Like I shocked her with a small electrical current. Like she's feeling everything I'm feeling. And I'd bet any amount of money she is.

It's sexual awareness. It's attraction. It's anticipation. She's made her choice. She doesn't have to tell me, or even admit it to herself, but she's made it nonetheless. I can feel it.

I walk her out to her car. My bike is parked sideways in front of it. She stops when we get close to it.

"Is this what you drive?" she asks, turning those wide eyes up to me.

"Yes," I say, but then I add with a smirk, "but you're not

surprised, are you? Isn't this what bad boys do? Ride motorcycles and break hearts?"

Her smile is weak. "I suppose so."

She turns away and moves around to unlock the car door and pop the hood.

I shouldn't have said that.

I unstrap the jumper cables I brought from behind the seat and hook them from my battery to hers.

"Will that be enough to jump-start my car?"

"Should be. Go give it a try."

I watch Olivia as she slides in behind the wheel to give it a crank. The engine doesn't turn over; it just makes a clicking sound.

She shakes her head and gets back out. "It's not working."

"You think?" I tease.

She tilts her head to the side and gives me a dirty look.

Damn, she's adorable.

"The reason for that is that it sounds like the alternator, not the battery."

She slumps over the car door. "Ohmigod! That's expensive, isn't it?" she mumbles.

"It's not cheap. But I know a guy." I say it in my best mobster voice.

She looks up and grins. "Those suspicious connections, huh? Can you get me some concrete boots while you're at it?"

"Probably," I say, deadpan.

I see a frown flicker across her forehead. She doesn't know whether I'm joking.

"Get your stuff. I'll take you home. I'll have my buddy come get your car and we'll figure something out tomorrow." She looks undecided, tapping her fingers along the door frame. "It'll be fine here for a little while. I don't think anybody will mess with it."

She snorts. And then looks embarrassed that she did. "In a way, I'd almost be relieved."

"Hey, I know a guy . . ." I say.

She laughs outright. And I love the sound. Makes me think of tickling her. In bed. While she's naked. Lying on top of me.

Without further argument, she locks up the car and comes to stand beside my bike. She shrugs her shoulders. "What now?"

"You've never ridden a motorcycle before?"

"Nope."

"What kind of bad-boy girlfriend are you?" I ask in mock dismay.

"Evidently a terrible one."

I swing onto the bike and grab my only helmet. "Nah, you just haven't met the right bad boy."

Her cheeks flush a little. I want to kiss her. Again. And I will. Just not right now.

"Put this on and then get on behind me," I say, handing her the helmet. Obediently, she slips it over her head and then throws one leg over the bike and scoots onto the seat. I see her long, bare legs clamp around my hips and I look back at her. Her eyes are shining behind the raised shield of the helmet as she situates herself against me. "Put your arms around my waist and hold on."

Her eyes never leaving mine, she leans in close and slides her hands around to my stomach. I can feel that plump chest of hers against my back and I jerk inside my jeans.

I turn around and start the engine. I let it idle for a few seconds while I regain my composure. It's hard to rid my mind of the image of her sitting in front of me, minus those shorts, with her legs wrapped around me. I'd give her the best ride home she's ever had.

With a growl, I rev the engine and ease us upright and off the kickstand. Shifting quickly into gear, we take off like a shot down the street.

I love the adrenaline of my bike. I always have. I try my best to let it chase away the feel of Olivia at my back, but I think nothing short of a week locked up in a bedroom with her can accomplish that. And oh, what a week that would be.

It doesn't take long to get to her place. It's kind of a sweet torture. In a way, I wish the ride were longer. But then, in another way, I'm glad it's not. The longer she's wrapped around me and pressed up against me, the harder it is to control myself. Especially now that I know she wants me.

And she's so close to giving in.

When I stop along the curb, she hesitates for a second before she gets off. She comes to stand beside me, handing me the helmet she's already removed. I hold it under my arm, against my leg, and wait for her to speak. She looks like she has something to say.

"How did you know where I live?"

She doesn't sound concerned. Just curious.

"Employee forms. Remember?"

"Ahh," she murmurs with a nod. She's waiting. And I think I know for what. "So, do you want to come in?"

"I'd better get back, but thanks, anyway."

She's good at hiding her disappointment. But not that good.

"Okay, well, thank you. I really appreciate you coming to help. And for the ride home, too, of course."

"Not a problem."

"So, I guess I'll talk to you tomorrow?"

"Yep. I'll be in touch."

She nods again, slowly. Waiting.

"Well, good night."

I love watching her, watching her uncertainty and her hesitation. And her attempts at denying what we both know she's feeling. Teasing her is going to be so much fun. Hot, sweet, sexy, delicious fun.

I reach out and brush her hair away from her cheek. "Sweet dreams, Olivia."

I rush to put my helmet on to hide my smile from her. I want her to be ready to beg for it.

TWENTY-ONE

Olivia

I walk away from Cash before I do something stupid like proposition him.

What the hell is the matter with you?

Before I get more than a few steps, I remember my car. I turn back to get Cash's attention before he pulls away. I dig my keys out and take them to him.

I see his frown behind the smoky shield of the helmet. "Don't you need them to get inside?"

"I've got a spare," I explain.

He nods once and takes the keys, sliding them into his front pocket.

I give him a quick smile, then hurry away. I refuse to look back at him, even though I know he's still at the curb. I can hear the throaty rumble of his idling bike. But more than that,

I can feel his eyes on me. I just wish they were his hands instead. And his mouth.

I shut my eyes as I reach for the spare key under the flower-pot on the small, covered porch. It's when I open my eyes to push it into the lock and open the door that I hear him accelerate away from the curb. I guess he was making sure I could get in okay without my keys.

Oh, good God! Don't show me the sweet, considerate side! I won't stand a chance.

After I get inside, I lean back against the door and stand there with my eyes closed until I can no longer hear even the faintest rumble of Cash's motorcycle.

My legs and butt are tingling from the vibrations of the bike. The rest of me is tingling from being wrapped around Cash. Tingling or aching. Or both.

Frustrated—both sexually and with myself for my utter lack of hormone control—I flick on the light and push away from the door. The first thing I see is the vase of flowers on the coffee table in the living room. They are a bright spot of color in an otherwise fairly muted room. I walk to the spray of lilies and bend to stick my nose into one. It smells wonderful, but something pokes the corner of my mouth. It's the card announcing who they're from.

I reach for the tiny square. I feel bad reading Marissa's "mail," but then again, she shouldn't leave it lying around. Or poking out of flower arrangements.

As I pull the card from the envelope, I chastise myself for inflicting more torture. I'm sure they're from Nash. And I'm sure the card is probably some sweet little love note that will make me want to jump out of a tall, tall building, but that doesn't stop me. I'm too curious, so I read it, anyway.

And I get a surprise.

> *Olivia, if you need anything, give me a call. I'm never far. N.*

A little thrill races down my spine. He must've used Marissa's keys to come inside and leave these for me. I can't help but wonder if he just dropped them off and left or if he stayed for a few minutes. Or walked around. Or went into my bedroom.

I doubt Nash would do anything like that, and the thought that he might ought to creep me out. Only it doesn't. The idea that he might've gone to look inside my bedroom excites me for some reason. And I'm already excited enough by his dangerous brother.

Feeling more and more like it's vibrator time, I get ready for bed. A vigorous tooth-brushing and face-scrubbing don't help that feeling. The brothers chase each other through my head, taunting me with their words and their eyes and their touch. By the time I slide between the sheets, I have no doubt what my dreams will be about. Or rather who my dreams will be about.

The click of the front door closing wakes me. Because I've just fallen asleep, it takes me a few seconds to determine whether I'm awake.

Strangely, I feel no fear when I see the tall, vague shadow

stop just outside my bedroom doorway. I recognize it instantly. I'd know that shape and that fluid way of moving anywhere.

It's Cash.

Or Nash.

I start to speak, but the words die on my lips when he moves slowly toward the bed. He stops at the foot. I've always loved how dark my room is until now. Now, I'd give anything to see him more clearly, for some clue as to which brother it is.

He bends and grabs the covers, dragging them off me. Chills spread over my arms and legs, partly due to the temperature change, partly due to the guy standing at the foot of my bed.

He says nothing. Neither do I. Instinctively, I know words will shatter the wicked perfection of the moment. And that's the last thing I want to do.

With very deliberate movements, he reaches forward and winds his long fingers around my ankles. Slowly, he pulls me toward him, toward the end of the bed. I'm breathless. And excited. And still I say nothing.

His fingers loosen their grip, but his hands don't leave me. No, instead, he slides his palms up the outsides of my calves to my knees, where he stops. I see him bend forward, and then I feel his lips on my left thigh. They're like a red-hot branding iron. His tongue flickers out to taste my skin, sending heat gushing to my core.

"I can't stop thinking about doing this to you," he whispers, so quietly I can barely hear him. "Tell me to stop now if you don't want this. If you don't want me."

Even as he speaks, his hands are skimming the outsides of

my thighs, sliding under the band of my panties. He pauses. Maybe he's waiting for me to tell him to go. Maybe he's rethinking what he's about to do. I have no idea because I don't know who's in my bed. And at the moment I don't care. I want both Cash and Nash. They both come with their own brand of trouble. Maybe not knowing which one I'm giving in to will be a good thing.

For tonight, I don't care. I don't think. I only want.

I feel his hands turn and his fingers curl around the elastic of my panties. He pauses a second time. I wonder again what he's thinking and what I can do to make him continue. My answer is to lift my hips off the bed. I hear air hiss through his teeth before he drags my panties down my legs. It must've been the answer he was looking for.

My chest is heaving with excitement when I feel his hands again, gliding up the insides of my thighs, pushing my legs apart. He puts one knee on the bed between mine and leans down, pressing his lips to my stomach.

"All I can think about is what you taste like," he murmurs, his tongue dipping into my navel, making my muscles clench in anticipation. "And what you feel like." I feel his palm cup me between my legs. I spread my thighs further. I'm rewarded with pure bliss when he slides a single finger inside me. He groans. "Oh my God, you're so wet." He pushes another finger into me. "All this for me," he whispers, moving his fingers in and out as I raise my hips to meet him.

His lips move down my belly and I feel his shoulders settle between my legs. His warm breath tickles me just before I feel the first stroke of his hot tongue. My back arches off the bed. "Mmm, even sweeter than I imagined," he moans, his fingers still moving inside me.

With lips and tongue, he licks and sucks until I feel the familiar tension of an orgasm building inside me. My hips move against him, grinding against his mouth as his fingers penetrate me harder and harder, faster and faster.

I fist my fingers in his hair, holding him to me when the world breaks apart. Light and heat explode behind my eyes and I cry out. I feel his hands come around my hips to hold me still and he finishes me off, burying his hot, wet tongue inside me, licking me from the inside.

My pulse is throbbing in every part of my body when I feel him move up to pull my tank top over my head. I'm limp beneath his hands when they cup my breasts, teasing the hard points of my nipples.

He draws one into his mouth, gently nibbling it with his teeth, intensifying the waves of pleasure coursing through me. I raise my hands to his shoulders and feel only smooth skin. He's not wearing a shirt.

I thread my fingers through his hair when he moves his head to my other breast. He teases and taunts it as well.

He moves again and his lips are on mine.

His tongue slips into my mouth to taunt mine, licking at it. I draw it into my mouth and close my lips around it, sucking gently. When I release it, I hear his hoarse whisper. "See how good you taste?" I cup his face and lap up the wetness from around his mouth, from down on his chin. He groans loudly, his body moving against mine. "That's right, baby. You like that, don't you?"

I hear his zipper followed by the rustle of his pants as he moves to push them down his legs. I use my heels to help him, reveling in the feel of his bare skin against the insides of my thighs.

He flexes his hips and I feel the tip of his hardness slip between my folds. He makes tiny movements, sliding back and forth, stroking me with his body. "Just so you know," he says breathlessly, "I'm clean. Tell me you are, too, and that you're on the pill," he begs.

"Yes," I answer breathlessly, the only word I've spoken since his arrival.

He comes up onto his elbows where he's poised above me. I can feel him looking down into my face even though I know he can't see me any better than I can see him. There is a smile in his voice when he says, "Perfect!"

And then slides into me.

I feel like whimpering when he stops far short of full penetration and pulls out again. I want to cry at the loss. But I don't have time. He moves in again, farther this time, letting me get used to his size before he pulls out once more. He continues to tease me, each time filling me up a little farther, bringing me closer to the edge again, until I'm ready to scream.

"Say it," he whispers, taunting me with the tip as he moves in and out in quick, short strokes. Reaching up, I fist my fingers in his hair and pull his mouth to mine. I use my lips and tongue to plead with him, to show him every ounce of my desire. I sink my teeth into his bottom lip and I lift my hips, hoping to bring him fully inside. But he pulls back, again only giving me part of himself. "Say it," he demands.

I'm panting with need, the threat of another orgasm tightening my muscles as I squeeze his hips between my legs, begging with my body. Still, he resists, never allowing his body to move more than a few inches into mine before retreating. "Say it," he repeats a third time.

I lick a trail from the base of his throat all the way to his ear, where I force out between shallow breaths the single word he wants to hear.

"Please."

As he bends his head, his mouth covers mine and he drives his body deep into mine, stealing my breath. He gives me every inch of length and girth as he moves violently within me, stretching me tight over and over again, driving me closer and closer to ecstasy.

His lips move over the skin of my face and neck to the valley between my breasts. Blood pumps to my tingling nipples when his mouth moves toward them. I arch my back, pressing my chest toward him, begging for the feel of his hot mouth and wet tongue. "Come for me," he says softly, drawing my nipple into his mouth and flicking it with his tongue. As if to punctuate his request, he grinds his hips into mine and bites down on my nipple. "Come for me, baby," he growls again.

It's all the motivation I need. Tightening around him, I give in to my second orgasm, glorying in the friction of his hips against mine as he rubs me into a wave of the purest pleasure.

I'm breathless as he pounds harder into me. I feel my body gripping his, milking it. His tempo increases with his breathing until, suddenly, he stiffens. "Olivia," he moans heavily, coming and spilling heat and passion deep inside me.

His movements slow, but he remains buried inside me, making the spasms of my body squeezing his even more pronounced. We remain like that for a couple of perfect minutes.

When neither of us has anything left to give, he collapses onto me and we lie in a tangle of damp limbs and heaving chests. With his weight braced on his forearms, he nestles his face in the curve of my neck and presses a soft, wet kiss to the skin beneath my ear. He says nothing, but his warm, heavy breath dries it.

My heart is filled with emotion, my head is spinning with questions, and my body is throbbing in the aftermath. There is so much to think about and worry over and contemplate, yet it seems so very . . . unimportant. Conflict rages inside me. In a thousand years, I would never have thought I could fall asleep like that.

But I do.

Dawn is just breaking when I open my eyes. Hot kisses and great sex are the first things that enter my mind.

I look around at my empty room. There's no evidence of any naughty nighttime visitors. In fact, I might've convinced myself I'd dreamed the whole thing if it weren't for the soreness I feel between my legs when I move.

I smile. It's a pleasant soreness, one that reminds me of the massive instrument that inflicted it.

Good God, did you just call it an instrument?

I giggle. I can't seem to help it. I'm happy. Very happy. At least for the moment.

I should be tired, but I'm not. I feel rejuvenated and ready to face the day.

"Maybe Ginger's right. Maybe sex is actually good for me," I mumble into the quiet. The walls absorb the sound and remind me that I have the place all to myself. Marissa is gone for another couple of weeks. That alone is reason to celebrate.

Thoughts of her bring me to thoughts of Nash. What if it had been him who visited me last night? I hadn't been able to see clearly enough in the dark to identify whether the delicious chest above me had a tattoo on it. How will I know?

For a moment, I'm lost in memories of the feel of smooth, taut skin beneath my fingertips, of rippling muscles in long arms and broad shoulders, of slim hips clamped between my thighs. Just the thought of that is enough to leave me feeling damp and wanting.

Throwing off the covers, I head to the shower. As I scrub and buff, I search my mind for clues that might hint at which brother gave me such an incredible night. I think they are both perfectly capable of making me feel that way, and nothing that happened seemed like something only one would do or say. Especially say, as not many words were used.

I smile at the thought.

Not many words were needed.

Entry isn't an issue. Cash has my keys; Nash has Marissa's. Attraction isn't an issue. Both brothers have made it very clear we have an intensely physical connection. Willingness might be the only area there's a discrepancy. Cash has made it very clear he's interested in a physical relationship with me. Nash, on the other hand, is taken and he's trying to do the right thing.

But then I remember it wasn't Nash who stopped us on the rooftop. If I hadn't brought us to a halt, would we have had sex up there, on a chaise longue where Nash has probably sat with Marissa?

The more I think, the muddier things get and the more questions and concerns I develop. So I put it out of my head. Surely I'll be able to tell when I see Cash whether we had sex.

Surely.

After dressing, I make my way into the kitchen to brew some coffee. I'm surprised when I hear my phone ring from my bedroom. I race to get it.

My stomach flutters when I see Nash's name on the lighted screen. What does such an early call mean? That he was with me until a little while ago? Or he got a good night's sleep, which means he wasn't here?

I slide my finger across the screen to answer it.

"Hello?"

There's a pause.

"Did I wake you?"

"No, I'm actually making coffee."

"Oh, good. I wouldn't want to disturb you. I assumed you'd have your alerts off and I'd get your voice mail. I just wanted to make sure you saw the flowers I left."

I'm a little deflated. That doesn't sound like something the guy who just explored my entire naked body with his tongue might say.

"Yes, I saw them when I came in last night."

"Perfect. I just wanted you to feel free to call me if you need anything while Marissa's away."

"Um, I will. Uh, thanks."

"I'll let you get back to your coffee, then. I've got to get to work. Early meetings."

"Okay. Thanks for the flowers, Nash."

"It was my pleasure, Olivia."

I hear a smile in his voice. Don't I?

Chills remain on my arms long after he hangs up. Just hearing him say my name reminds me of the night before, of that voice moaning my name as he was coming.

Only it obviously didn't belong to Nash. It belonged to his brother.

I'm not entirely surprised to find out it was Cash. The whole scenario fits his character more than it does Nash's. Only a bad boy would come, uninvited, into a girl's house and wake her up to seduce her in her own bedroom.

And only a bad boy would think I wouldn't mind. I have to smile.

He's got nerve. I'll give him that.

But he was right. I didn't mind. In fact, I didn't mind twice.

And probably wouldn't have minded a third and fourth time if I hadn't fallen asleep like a loser. It's been a while and I forgot how incredibly relaxing great sex is.

I'm just sitting down at the dining room table to do some reading before class when my phone rings again. This time the screen shows Cash's name, but my reaction is the same. My stomach flutters with excitement.

"Hello?"

"Good morning, gorgeous. You up?"

"Yep," I say, unable to keep the grin from my voice.

"So, your car is at my buddy's shop. It's definitely the alternator."

"Shit," I mumble, my early-morning buzz succumbing to the realities of owning a piece-of-crap car. "Any idea how much something like that's gonna cost me?"

"For you? Nothing. He owes me a favor."

"I can't let you do that, Cash."

"I suppose you're going to stop me?" he says derisively.

"I'm being serious. That's too much. I can't accept a gift like that."

"You can and you will. Besides, don't think of it as a gift. You'll be paying me back."

My smile returns and my nerves sing with exhilaration. I can't wait to hear what he has in mind.

"Is that right?"

"Yep. Starting with an extra shift next week if you can swing it."

I'm disappointed again. That's not nearly as sexy as I

expected it to be. After last night, surely he knows I'd be more than happy to pay him back in any number of ways and positions. Unless he's not my late-night visitor after all.

What kind of a floozy doesn't know who she slept with the night before?

I roll my eyes.

And who uses the word floozy?

One name comes to mind. Tracey, my mother. That's her word.

Shaking my head, I get back to important things. Like who spent part of last night tickling my ovaries.

As I think about it, the thing that bothers me most is that neither guy is amorous enough this morning for me to be able to accurately determine the culprit. How sad is that?

Ohmigod! Have I lost my touch? Do I suddenly suck in bed?

Cash's clearing his throat reminds me he's awaiting my answer.

"Oh, uh, you know I'll do whatever I can to pay you back, but it kinda depends on the night. I can't be out too—"

"Oh, you won't be out very late. This is an accounting project I'd like you to look at. I just ask that you don't put your hair in a bun or wear orthopedic shoes."

I laugh at his vision. "Fine. I guess I can work my numeric magic without the tools of my trade."

"I'm sure you can," he says absently. "In the meantime, however, you'll need a ride to school, right?"

"Um, yeah." I didn't even think of that. These guys have really scrambled my brain. "I guess I will."

"Give me ten minutes and I'll be there to get you."

My brain finally starts working and I begin to think like a rational person. If Cash takes me to school, I'll have no way home unless I call a taxi, which will get expensive since I'll have to take one to work and back all weekend until my car gets fixed.

"You know, I can skip school today. It's not like I'm taking any really hard classes now, anyway. That way I won't have to impose on you any more than I already have."

"You're not imposing on me. I don't mind."

"I'd really rather not bother you. Really. I'll just see you tonight."

"Get dressed. Be ready. I'll be there in ten."

With that, he hangs up, giving me no choice in the matter.

Almost exactly ten minutes later, I hear the deep rumble of Cash's bike. I feel it in my stomach, like it breathed excitement into my body in a very physical way. Try as I might to keep my distance from him, it's clear I'm getting into a bad place with Cash.

And the worst part of it is, I don't think I want to stop.

I don't wait for him to come to the door. Rather, I go out to meet him, carefully locking the door behind me.

Cash is straddling his glossy black-and-chrome bike. His jeans—blue for a change—are stretched tight across his thighs and his plain white tee is snug over his chest. His dark blond hair is disheveled, as always, making my fingers itch to run through it. But it's his face that makes me catch my breath. He's more handsome than any guy I've ever seen in real life, and there's something about his eyes and his smile today that seem to sear the air between us, setting it on fire.

And even though I know the risk, I want to jump headfirst into the flames.

TWENTY-TWO

Cash

Something about the look on her face makes me feel like a meal. And if I were, I'd be a happy meal, for sure. Although I'm still impatient, I'm relieved. I figured she'd come around eventually. I knew she wouldn't be able to fight what's between us for too long. It's too strong.

And tempting.

"You keep looking at me like that and you're gonna have a big surprise to deal with when you get on this bike," I tell her.

"A big surprise?" she asks, a mischievous smile tugging at the corners of her mouth. "Nah, don't you mean something more like a Tic Tac?"

I love her sense of humor. It's a little shy, just like her, and it pokes its head out at the most unusual times.

I smile and hold out my hand to her. "Then come here and let me freshen your breath."

She laughs. And, as always, I want to do something immediately to make her laugh again. She thinks too much, worries too much. I don't know about what, but I can see it nonetheless. It makes me want to brighten her mood and give her as many carefree minutes as I can.

Carefree and pleasurable.

I stifle a groan.

She puts her hand in mine and holds on to it as she straddles the seat behind me. Without turning around, I pass her the helmet. In the sideview mirror, I watch her slip it onto her head. There's something so sexy about seeing her in a helmet. Probably something about the way it makes me picture her in black, skintight leather, leaning forward on my bike with me behind her, my hands on her hips . . .

I grit my teeth. Damn her and that lush body of hers!

I reach back and curl my fingers behind each of her knees and pull her forward. I *feel* more than *hear* her gasp as her crotch snugs up against my hips and her chest flattens against my back.

I feel satisfied that now she's probably as highly attuned to me as I am to her, but then she ups the ante. She winds her arms around my waist and lets her hands ride dangerously low on my stomach. They're resting right above my buckle. Right above where she'll soon feel my hard-on if she's not careful. I take a deep breath before I put the bike into gear and accelerate away from the curb.

I can't get her to school fast enough.

As we get close to campus, she points ahead to which roads and turns to take to get her near where she needs to be. When we arrive, I pull along the curb and stop, dropping my feet to the ground to stabilize the bike while she dismounts. She stands facing me to take off the helmet. When she does, she shakes her dark hair free. It looks like something a girl in a shampoo commercial might do. I have no doubt she doesn't have a clue how sexy she is. But she is. Holy hell, is she ever!

She holds out the helmet to me, her eyes on mine. When I don't take it, she glances down at it and back up to me in question. I stand, still straddling the bike, and brush the helmet away, instead running my hands through her long hair and pulling her mouth to mine.

Although she's obviously surprised, she doesn't hold back. She kisses me like she means it. Like she wants more. All she'd have to do is say the word and I'd drive her straight back home and we'd spend the day in bed. But when I pull away and look into her wide eyes, I know it's still a little too soon for that. She's close, but she's not quite ready.

I can wait. I'll have to.

"When are you gonna say yes?"

She says nothing as she watches me with her deep emerald eyes. Her lips are red and puffy, and slightly parted as she breathes shallowly.

I smile. Oh yeah, it won't be long.

"Call me when you're ready for me to come get you," I say, giving her a quick peck on the lips before I put on the helmet. She looks dazed, which makes me want to smile. "Don't worry. You don't have to say yes today. I'll wait. You'll be worth it." Before I lower the shield over my face, I grin and wink at her. "And so will I."

I pull off down the street. When I look into the sideview mirror, I see that she's still standing exactly where I left her, staring after me.

TWENTY-THREE

Olivia

It's official. Cash is in my head. I may be present *physically* for all my classes, but it doesn't do me one bit of good. The only thing I learn is that he kisses like a tornado that's hell-bent on ruining my life.

I still don't know who was in my room last night, but I'm starting to genuinely hope it was Cash and not Nash. Yes, Nash is everything I *should* want in a man, everything my mother tried to drum into my head. Not to mention that he's hotter than seven shades of hell and could probably make me forget my convictions when he kisses me.

But beside Cash . . . he's beginning to pale in comparison.

I don't know if it's my inherent love of the sexy bad boy or if it's that Cash is turning out to be *more* than what I initially thought. Either way, he's in my head. Under my skin. And I doubt I'll be able to resist him much longer.

Don't get me wrong. He's still dangerous and will probably break my heart. And I'll try to hold out as long as I can. But in my heart, in my gut, I know there's something between us that won't go away until we sweat it out of each other.

The fun way.

But the way that will end with me in tears, watching him leave.

At least this time, it's a *choice*, though. It's *my* choice. I'm going into it knowing full well that might happen. I might not be able to keep from getting hurt, but I'm in control enough to make the choice for myself.

And, in the end, I'll choose Cash. Try as I might to fight it, it's inevitable. If only he could be a little, teeny, tiny bit like Nash . . .

My phone jars me from my thoughts. I forgot to turn the ringer off. I jump, scrambling to dig it out of my bag and answer it before I get crucified by my professor.

I reach for the button on the side to mute it and am getting ready to slip it back into my bag when I see Ginger's name on the screen. With a shrug, I pick up my book and my bag and head for the door. I've already disrupted class and I'm not learning a thing, anyway. I might as well just go ahead and leave.

When I hit the talk button, I'm greeted by Ginger's raised, irate voice and a long string of profanity. "Stay in your lane, you limp-dick, candy-ass, crazy motherfu—"

"Ginger?" I interrupt.

She quiets immediately. "Oh, Liv. Hi, sweetie. I didn't hear you answer."

"I can't imagine why," I remark dryly. "What's up?"

"Well, actually, I'm on my way to get you."

"Me? Why?" The hair at my nape prickles with unease. If Ginger is on her way to get me, something's wrong.

"Because your car is broken again, right?"

"Um, yes, but how did you know?"

"You had to have someone drive you all the way to Salt Springs for your last shift, remember?"

Nash. "Oh, right. But it's been fixed since then."

"Well hell," she says in frustration. "But wait, you just said it's broken."

"I know. It is. It's just a different break."

"Liv, seriously, I fear for your life in that piece of shit. No car should tear up as frequently as yours does. Do you have Munchausen's by proxy?"

"Munchausen's by proxy?"

"Yeah, you know where people, like, poison their family members and stuff for attention."

"I know what it is. I'm just a little surprised you do."

I can hear the proud smile in her voice. "I saw a special on the Discovery Channel."

"*You* were watching the Discovery Channel?"

"Yes."

"Um, why?"

"I lost the remote."

"You lost the remote?"

"Yes. Are you just gonna repeat everything I say?"

"If you keep saying ridiculously unbelievable things, then yes, probably."

"What have I said that's ridiculous?"

"That I might have Munchausen's by proxy. With my car. That you learned something on the Discovery Channel. That you even know what the Discovery Channel is. And that you sat in your living room watching a show about Munchausen's syndrome because you lost the remote control. How can you lose the remote control in a house as small as yours?"

"It was in the freezer. Apparently when I took out the vodka, I set the remote control down."

"That makes sense," I say sarcastically.

"The batteries in that bitch'll probably never die now," she says with a bark of laughter.

"Ginger, can I ask you a question?" I ask gently.

"Sure, sweetie. What is it?"

"Why are you on your way to get me?"

Sometimes Ginger needs a little redirection to stay on point. Sometimes I need the same thing when I'm *with* Ginger.

"Oh, damn! It's your dad. He fell and broke his leg. He made me promise not to tell you, but . . . well, you know. I'm gonna. Of course, I'm gonna."

"He broke his leg? When?"

"Two days ago."

"And I'm just now finding out about this?"

I have to concentrate on keeping my voice lowered. I'm intensely annoyed that I'm finding out so long after the fact.

"I wasn't going to tell you at all. He made me promise, you know. Like I said. But then when Tad mentioned seeing him at the hospital and that he's expecting some lambs, well, I knew you'd want to know. Someone who knows what the hell they're doing will have to come take care of things for a day or two until you find the babies and whatever else you need to do."

"So if there weren't lambs on the way, no one would've told me?"

My anger is rising.

"Uh," Ginger says quietly, knowing she's on dangerous ground. "That fool father of yours made everyone promise. He doesn't want you having to make the trip home or spend your time worrying about him."

I pinch the skin between my eyes, wishing I could stop the dull throb that's building across the front of my head. I bite back the dozen or so sharp comments that are trembling on the tip of my tongue.

"How far out are you?"

"About ten minutes."

"I'm still at school. You'll have to pick me up here."

"That's fine. Just give me directions."

I sigh. Loudly. Trying to give Ginger directions and then expecting her to actually show up at the correct location is a lot like throwing a knife into the air. It's dangerous and stupid, and somebody could end up getting hurt. She has landed us in questionable parts of town more than once, places I would never dream of getting out of the car. Unless, of course, I was accompanied by two ninjas and a sumo wrestler.

But in this case, what choice do I have? I wouldn't feel comfortable imposing on either Cash or Nash. It wouldn't be such a big deal if I could use Magic Vagina powers, but those only work on people a girl has slept with. And since I still have no clue which brother dove headfirst into my panties last night, there can be no wielding of the Magic Vagina.

I give Ginger directions to the student center. At least I can get something to drink while I wait for her.

After we hang up, I call Cash to tell him I won't be able to work the weekend shift.

"I'm so sorry, but it's a family emergency."

"I understand. Do you want me to come get you now?"

"No, my friend Ginger is on her way."

There's a long pause. "I would've taken you wherever you needed to go."

"I appreciate that, but she was already on her way when she called."

"Hmmm," is his only response.

"Well, thank you so much for . . . everything. I promise I'll take care of stuff with my car when I get back. And I'll pick up as many extra shifts as you need me to in order to make this up."

I hate the thought of losing my new job and having to go crawling back to my old one, but it's my dad . . .

"Don't worry about that. We'll figure something out. You're not going to be out of a job when you get back, if that's what you're thinking."

I close my eyes in relief. The thought had very much crossed my mind.

"I really appreciate your understanding," I say, injecting into my voice all the sincerity I can muster.

"I'm sure I can think of some way for you to pay me back."

The comment is wildly inappropriate, of course, but I can hear the smile in Cash's voice. He's teasing me.

"I'm sure you can. The question is: Can you think of something that does *not* involve me taking off my clothes?"

I'm playing with fire and I know it.

"Of course! Wear a skirt and only one item will need to come off. I'd just hate for you to miss out on . . . everything else."

A little shiver works its way down my spine and lands in the pit of my stomach like a bolt of lightning. I laugh uncomfortably. I can't tease like he can.

He must know I'm at a loss. He chuckles. "Take care of what you need to. Take your time. Call if you need anything."

"I will. And thanks, Cash."

After we hang up, I get a drink from the taco joint inside the student center and then walk back outside to sit on one of the benches and await Ginger. I wonder if I should call Nash. Just to let him know I won't be in town all weekend. He might want to keep an eye on things.

Or at least that's what I tell myself. The excuse I use.

"Nash, it's Olivia," I say when he answers.

I hear his soft laugh. "I know who you are, Olivia."

I feel the blush sting my cheeks. I'm glad he can't see it. "Oh, right. Sorry." I clear my throat nervously. "So, I'll be out of town for the weekend. I just wanted you to know in case . . . well, just in case anybody needed anything."

Ohmigod, could you sound any more lame?

"Okay. Thanks for letting me know. Need some time away from my overbearing brother already?"

I know he's teasing, but I don't like that he puts Cash down. "He's not overbearing. And no, it's nothing like that. I need to go home for the weekend. That's all."

The lightness evaporates from his tone, replaced by concern. "Is everything all right?"

"Yeah. My father broke his leg. He's fine, it's just that he was expecting some lambs and he can't get out with a broken leg to find and check on them, so . . ."

"Is that something you can do by yourself? Do you need some help?"

"Nah, I grew up on that farm, helping him until I was old enough to do things by myself. I'll be fine. But thank you for asking."

What a great guy! Dammit!

"Well, if you need some help, you know where to find me."

"Thanks, but I could never ask you to do that."

"Olivia, please," he begins. The way he says my name makes my stomach squeeze. It sounds so much like it did last night. Was it his lips I kissed? His touch I felt? "Ask. If you need help, I want to know."

"Okay," I say, already feeling a bit breathless. Too breathless to argue, anyway. "I will."

"Good. I'll keep an eye on the place until you get back. Give me a call when you arrive."

"Will do. Thanks, Nash."

"You bet."

The brothers alternate taking up space in my head, like they so often do, as I await Ginger. I just don't know when it will get any easier with them. Or even if it *will*.

I'm still preoccupied when I hear a horn honking and someone shouting my name at the top of her lungs.

It's Ginger.

"No effin' way," I say under my breath as I make my way to her car. She's standing in the driver's seat, hanging out the sunroof. By the time I get to her, she's smiling like an escaped mental patient.

"Bet you thought I'd get lost, didn't you?"

I say nothing. I *totally* thought she'd get lost. In fact, I'd have guaranteed it.

Of course, I'd have been wrong. Maybe that's my new streak—being wrong. Maybe I'm wrong about a lot of things. Things I'd *love* to be wrong about.

If only I could be that lucky . . .

Ginger doesn't wait long to stir up interesting conversation. "So, did you take the penis challenge?"

"Ginger!"

"Olivia! You better have news for me. And details. It's been a while for me."

"Yeah, right. What's 'a while'? A week?"

She glances at me, clearly horror-stricken. "Good God, no! It's only been four days. But I've got needs."

"Ginger, I'm pretty sure you're a freak of nature."

"Heavy on the freak, sweetie," she adds cheekily.

I laugh. That's one thing about Ginger. She doesn't try to hide who she is or what she likes. She owns her every wart and pimple with pride. And she wears them each flawlessly.

"You would die of boredom in my body."

"No, I'd take that young thing out for a spin and liven things up a little."

I roll my eyes. "I'm sure you would. You'd have me screwing my way through greater Atlanta."

"Breakin' hearts and blowin' minds! Or blowin' something," she says with a devilish wink.

"Oh, Lord!" I shake my head. She's incorrigible. She's also practically impossible to insult. Obviously.

"Now, stop changing the subject. Did you do it?"

I can't hide the smile that tugs at my lips. She's too observant.

She points animatedly at me. "You did! You did! How was it? Which one was better? And when will the other one be coming to visit me?"

"Well, that's the thing. I'm not exactly sure which one I slept with."

I cringe when I see her turn wide, shocked eyes on me. Ginger also happens to be nearly unshockable. The fact that I've managed it can't possibly be a good sign.

"How does that even happen?"

I go through the story. The short, less detailed version, of course. When I'm finished, she starts laughing. Hard.

"Well, you know what you have to do now, right?"

"I'm *not* asking them, if that's what you're about to suggest."

"Oh, hell no. I was just gonna say you *have* to sleep with

them both now. It's the only way you'll be able to tell who owns the enchanted tongue." Ginger turns a wicked smile on me. "Oh, poor you. Forced to have vagina-exploding sex with hot twins. Oh, please no! Anything but that!"

"If it were just that, it'd be fine, but you know I can't . . . I don't . . ."

I'm picking at my fingernails, but still, from the corner of my eye, I see Ginger look at me.

"This isn't about that jackhole Gabe, is it?"

"You know Gabe has nothing to do with—"

"Bullshit! Liv, you've got to get over that. Just because a guy looks or dresses or acts a certain way doesn't mean he's just like Gabe. And, by the same token, just because a guy *doesn't* look, dress, or act like him doesn't mean he's not. You can't judge all books by that emotionally stunted, dimwitted, tiny-dicked prick's cover. You can't stop taking chances in life just because you got burned."

I think of my earlier decision to take the risk with Cash. But I also think of how amazingly supportive and considerate Nash was when I called. If Ginger's right, despite their outward appearances, either one could be Gabe all over again. But how will I ever know which one is and which one isn't?

Or maybe they both are.

Go with your gut. Go with what you know. Nash is the good guy. Cash is the bad boy. Bad boys don't change their spots.

But Nash is taken.

Cash is not.

Nash is offering me nothing.

173

Cash wants to be honest and give me what he's capable of.

Is it worth it to have either of them in my life? Or would I be better off to turn my back on both of them? And run.

Sensing my mood, Ginger changes the subject to a much less upsetting one—sex toys.

Oh, Ginger!

I'm pretty shocked when I walk through the front door and see a hospital bed in the living room. My heart drops onto the hardwood with a thud only I can hear.

When I see my father sitting in his favorite old green recliner with his white-casted leg resting on a pillow, I feel minimally relieved, albeit still confused. The cast is not on the lower half of his leg, like I expected. It goes all the way up to his hip.

My father broke his femur. And no one told me.

Damn it to hell!

I drop my bags on the floor and go straight to him, hands on hips, fully armed with righteous indignation.

"And you couldn't have called to tell me? You let me find out *days* later from *Ginger*, of all people?"

I can see by the look in his hazel eyes that he's slipping into feather-smoothing mode. It's that desire to avoid confrontation that eventually drove my mother to leave and find greener, stronger pastures. And richer pastures. And more successful pastures. Basically any other pasture than the one she was grazing in. The cow!

Sometimes it's all I can do not to hate her.

"Now, punk," he begins, using my childhood pet name, the one that always turns me to putty in his hands. "You know I'd never keep something from you unless I knew it was best for you. You've got so much on your plate with this new job and with your last year of school and living with your cousin, I would never want to add to your load. Try to see it from my perspective," he finishes sweetly.

It's impossible to be mad when he does this. I must admit it can be very frustrating, though.

I drop to my knees at his feet. "Dad, you should've called."

"Liv, there's nothing you could've done. Except worry. And now you're missing work. Because of me."

"It's not a big deal. Ginger mentioned the lambs. I'll get them squared away and be back to work in no time."

He closes his eyes and leans his head back, rolling it back and forth over the headrest in exasperation. He says nothing for a few seconds, effectively ending this portion of the conversation.

It's another frustrating habit of his. He just stops. Stops talking, stops discussing. Just . . . stops.

I notice a few more gray hairs at his temples than I'd seen last time. And it seems the brackets that frame his mouth are deeper. Today, he looks so much older than his forty-six years. His hard, disappointing life has always taken a toll. And now it's showing.

"What can I do to help, Dad? I'm here, so you might as well put me to work. How are the books?"

He doesn't look at me, but he answers. "The books are fine.

I've been having Jolene help me with them in between your visits."

I grit my teeth. Jolene thinks she's an accountant. Only she's not. Not by a long shot. I'm sure there's a mess to clean up. I feel a sigh coming on, so I change the subject.

"What about the house? Is there anything that needs doing around here?"

Finally, he raises his head and looks at me. There's humor in his eyes. "I'm a grown man, Liv. I know how to make do without my daughter here to take care of me."

I roll my eyes. "I know that, Dad. That's not what I'm saying and you know it."

He reaches forward and grabs a chunk of hair near my ear. He tugs on it, just like he used to tug on my pigtails when I was little. "I knew what you meant. But I also know you think you have to take care of me, especially since your mother left. But you don't, hon. It would kill me to see you put your life on hold to come back here. Go find a better life somewhere else. That's what would make me happy."

"But, Dad, I don't—"

"I know you, Olivia Renee. I raised you. I know what you're planning and how you think. And I'm asking you not to do this. Just leave me be in this life. There's something different out there for you. Something better."

"Dad, I love these sheep and this farm. You know that."

"I'm not saying you don't. And we'll always be here for you to come visit. And one day, when I'm gone, this will all be yours, to do with as you like. But for now, it's mine. My problem, my life, my worry. Not yours. Your worry is to graduate and get a good job so you can buy your old man out ten times over. Then maybe I'll think about letting you come back home. How's that sound?"

I know what he's doing, what he's getting at. And I understand it. I understand guilt. But when I nod my head and smile in agreement, it's only for his benefit. What he doesn't know is that I will never leave him like she did. Never. I'll never choose a cushy life of means over the people I love. Never.

"Now, since you're already here, I have a favor. Well, two, actually."

"Name it."

"I've got all the fixin's for chuckwagon beans. Will you put some on for supper?"

"They're your favorite. Of course I will."

"Good girl."

He smiles at me for a few seconds, then turns his attention back to the show he was watching on television.

"Dad?"

"Huh?" he asks, looking back at me, eyebrows raised.

"What was the second favor?"

He frowns for a second, and then his face lights up. "Oh! Oh, right. Ginger and Tad are wanting you to come by tonight for your belated farewell party."

I start shaking my head. "I'm not leaving you to go to a—"

"Yes, you are. The game comes on tonight. I'd like to watch it in peace while you have some laughs with your friends. Is that too much for a wounded old man to ask of his daughter?"

I snort. "Like I'm gonna say no after you put it that way."

Again, I know what he's doing. And why. But I'll go along with this one, only because I know how much he loves football and he genuinely probably wants to watch it by himself, without me fussing about his blood pressure when he gets all worked up and yells at the screen.

His smile is satisfied when he turns back to the television a second time. This time, I leave him to go start supper.

A series of whistles greet me as I walk through the door at Tad's, making me tug self-consciously at my skirt. That's the bad thing about not having time to pack a bag. It leaves me stuck with the clothes in my closet at home, clothes I outgrew a couple of years ago.

My black skirt is shorter than I'd like, and the T-shirt I'm wearing with it is a bit more . . . formfitting than it needs to be, not to mention I don't ever remember it showing so much belly. If I weren't an adult, Dad probably wouldn't have let me leave the house until I changed. Unfortunately, yoga pants or cut-off jean shorts with paint on them were my only other options, so short skirt and tight shirt it is.

It doesn't take me long to settle into the comfort of the familiar. Drinks flow freely and there's more of a party atmosphere than usual. It's not long before my head is spinning happily, warning me I need to slow down on the drinks.

I'm laughing with Ginger, who took the shift off to sit on the other side of the bar with me tonight, when I see the door open behind her. My heart squeezes painfully when I see my ex, Gabe, walk in with his girlfriend, Tina, on his arm.

He looks the same as always—dangerously handsome with his jet-black hair, pale blue eyes, and cocky, to-die-for smile. He even has the same issues as before—a girl on his arm and a wandering eye. He doesn't even try to hide the fact that he's checking out other girls. And Tina, God love her, she just pretends not to notice. Talk about dysfunction!

Ginger, having noticed my silent, openmouthed stare, turns to look. "Oh sweet heaven, who let that bastard in?"

She turns and starts to slide off her stool as if to rectify the situation. Reaching out, I put my hand on her arm, stopping her from getting up. "Don't. It's not worth it."

Actually, I'd love to see her kick his ass out, but it would only make me look more pathetic, so I'd rather just drink enough to drown him out of my consciousness.

I signal Tad, who is working a rare shift behind the bar tonight to cover for Ginger's absence, and ask him to bring us another round of shots. That's the fastest way to oblivion as far as I'm concerned. And oblivion is looking very appealing at the moment.

Ginger and I toast one another and down the shots. I feel the burn of eighty proof all the way to my stomach, where it kindles a warm fire. She whoops excitedly and I laugh at her, but my eyes can't help but stray back out to the crowd in search of Gabe.

When they find him, he's sitting down at a tall table. Despite the girl at his side, his eyes find me. In them, there's recognition.

And hunger, just like there always was. And I react instantly, just like I always did. Only now, the reaction dies almost immediately, the flames doused by the cold waters of reality and how he's here tonight with Tina rather than with me.

I'd listened to his lies for months, falling more deeply in love with him by the day, when all the while, he'd had a girlfriend he'd never had any intention of leaving. The worst part was, they have a son together. They were basically a family. And even though they'd never actually split, he'd made me feel like a homewrecker. He'd made me feel like my mother. And for that, he doesn't deserve my forgiveness.

I try to enjoy the rest of the night, enjoy a farewell gathering with my old friends and coworkers, but my mood continues to darken. Every drink and every laugh seems tainted, tainted by the presence of the umpteenth bad boy I'd fallen for.

Ginger orders us another round of shots, which I gladly accept even though I know I'm pushing my limit, and we toss them back amid the cheers of our friends. The alcohol is just starting to burn off my bitterness when someone at the door catches my attention again.

This time, Cash strolls in.

TWENTY-FOUR

Cash

I'm not surprised by anything I see when I walk into the sports bar. It's typical, with its dozen or so televisions lining the walls and a collection of tables in the center of the room facing them. The bar is to my right followed by four pool tables, crouching under long Budweiser lights. Beyond those is a small dance floor.

Within seconds, my eyes find Olivia. It's like they're drawn to her. When I see her sitting at the bar with her friends, I know two things are true. One, she'll be drunk if she doesn't stop drinking soon. And two, I'll have that skirt pushed up around her waist before the night's out.

When her eyes meet mine, I see resistance in them. I've seen it before, but I thought we'd pretty much moved past that. I can't help but wonder what has happened since this morning to set her back.

There's an expletive resting on my tongue, but I bite it back and keep my face neutral as I walk toward her. When I stop beside her, I watch her straighten her spine and tip her chin up. Yep, resistance. And she's determined.

Even though it frustrates me, I find it pretty freakin' hot. It makes me want to *make* her want me despite all the reasons she thinks she shouldn't.

So I will.

Again.

"I would ask if I could buy you a drink, but it looks like you've already had a few too many."

"I already have one father. He's at home nursing a broken leg, thank you very much," she says with a bit of a slur.

"No offense intended. Just an observation." I signal the bartender, who is watching me with nothing less than hostility. "Jack. Neat." I'm in her territory now. She's among her friends and they're obviously very protective. The strange thing is that they'd feel the need to protect her from me, even though they've never met me.

Damn, I guess she really does have a weakness for a certain type. And all her friends must know about it.

It irritates the shit out of me that she's pigeonholed me, as have all her friends. There's nothing I hate worse than to be judged unfairly. Not one of these people knows the first thing about me, Olivia included.

It would be interesting to see how she'd react if she knew

everything, knew the truth. In just a few short sentences, I could give her every reason in the world to run away from me as far and as fast as she can. But I won't. Because I'm feeling selfish. I don't want her to run away yet. I need more from her first.

A lot more.

When the bartender sets a glass in front of me, I toss him a ten and down my drink in one gulp. I nod for another and slide my empty glass back.

I make a point to ignore Olivia as I stand awaiting my next drink. Finally, she speaks. I almost smile. I wanted her to make the first move. And she did.

"What are you doing here?" she asks, scooting off her stool to stand beside me. I wonder if it makes her feel more in control, more in charge to be standing.

Or maybe it makes her feel safer, like she can get away quickly. Run.

"I thought you might need some help. So I came to help."

I see her eyes flicker to her right for a split second before returning to me.

"How did you find me?"

"My brother."

"No, I mean how did you know I was here?"

"Your father."

"You went to my *house*?"

She's obviously perturbed about that. "Yes. Is that a problem? Are visitors not welcome at your secret lair?"

I watch, fascinated, as anger stiffens her muscles. She props her fists on her hips. Damn, she's fiery. "Did it ever occur to you that maybe you should wait until you're invited?"

"If I were invited, then I wouldn't be volunteering, now would I?"

Even in her agitation, I see her glance for the second time to a table at her right. I follow her gaze to a guy sitting there with a mousy-looking girl. The way he's watching Olivia leaves me with no doubt that they know each other. And very well by the looks of it.

I take a step closer to Olivia and lean down to ask quietly, "Is that the guy?"

She jerks her head toward me, guiltily. Angrily. "What guy? What are you talking about?"

"Oh come on. Admit it. That's the last bad boy, isn't it?" I look back at the douche who is inadvertently making my life more difficult. "Looks like he recovered from the wood chipper pretty well. Want me to kick his ass?"

I look back to Olivia. A range of emotions flit across her face, beginning with confusion and ending in something close to humor, to a smile.

"No, I don't want you to kick his ass."

"You sure? Because I specialize in deassholization."

This time she smiles. "Deassholization?"

"Yeah. Just think of me as the Orkin man of assholes—putting assholes in their place."

"Well, I appreciate the offer, but he's not worth it."

I reach forward to tuck a stray lock of raven hair behind her ear. "If he hurt you, he's worth it."

I really don't think Olivia knows how expressive her face is. I can plainly see that she's affected by me, that she likes me and probably wouldn't argue if I stripped her down and licked her from head to toe, even though letting me would be against her better judgment. But I can also see that she doesn't *want* to feel those things. She wants to be ambivalent, unaffected. She wants to be impervious to me. Only she's not. And, if I can help it, she *won't be*, either.

I recognize the lively song that comes on. "Ho Hey" would never be played at my club, mainly because it *is* a club, but I like it nonetheless. The words have me feeling a little sentimental toward the confused and gun-shy Olivia.

"Come on, then," I say, taking Olivia by the hand. "Let's go rub it in."

I reach for her friend's hand, too, the lady who's been watching me since I walked in, like I'm a potential snack. "I'm Cash, Olivia's boss. Come dance with us."

"Ginger," she declares with a broad smile. She wraps her fingers around mine, giving me zero resistance.

As I tow the girls across the bar toward the dance floor, Ginger is drumming up attention, which is perfect for what I have in mind. "Come on, y'all. Let's give Liv a farewell dance she'll never forget."

Within seconds, there are two dozen of Olivia's biggest fans surrounding us on the dance floor, singing along and showering her with smiles and hugs and attention. I can see her face light up, her demeanor relax.

She looks back at that other guy only one time, and even

then, it's almost an absentminded kind of thing. For the most part, her focus is concentrated on the people around her. And on me.

I can see the ice melting each time her eyes meet mine. When I smile, she smiles in return. When I reach for her hand, she laces her fingers through mine. And when she turns to me, it looks as though, at least for the time being, she's stopped lumping me in with the d-bag who she wishes had fallen into a wood chipper.

Her eyes are sparkling and happy, and she appears to be genuinely pleased. "Thank you for this. You're a very talented agent of deassholization."

"Oh, this isn't my method of choice. Trust me. But if it makes you happy, then I'm okay with it."

She looks away shyly, but her eyes come back to mine, unable to resist the magnetism that's between us. "Well, it makes me very happy."

"Then let's finish him off, shall we?"

She quirks one eyebrow and smiles. I see the daring girl rise to the surface. She's feeling like she can take on the world, conquer anything including an ex-boyfriend.

She's ready to jump. And I'm ready to catch her.

"What did you have in mind?" she asks coyly, licking her lips.

I look around and locate the signage for the bathrooms. I smile down at her, taking both her hands in mine and backing out of the crowd, toward the restrooms. I don't take my eyes off her.

Her cheeks are flushed and her eyes are wide with excitement. She doesn't know what I have in mind, but I think *she thinks* it's risqué. And she seems okay with that, which makes me even bolder.

Not once does she glance at that guy's table as we pass, but I see him from the corner of my eye. He says something to the girl he's with and he gets up to leave. He looks angry, which makes me smirk.

When we reach the short hallway outside the bathrooms, I pull Olivia to me and kiss her. She's warm and pliant, and within seconds, she's working her fingers into my hair and pressing her chest against mine.

I was only planning to kiss her where that asshole could see us, but Olivia isn't thinking about him anymore.

Now neither am I.

The music fades around us when she bends her knee and rubs her leg against mine. I reach down and run my fingers up the smooth skin of her calf. She reaches down and puts her hand on top of mine, guiding it to her hip. Happy to oblige, I cup her perfect ass in my hand and squeeze.

Her moan tickles along my tongue and vibrates to my lower half to stiffen everything from my waist down. When the kiss that was supposed to be more a tease than anything else turns rough with passion, I stop thinking about everything but the girl in my arms.

I reach behind me and twist the doorknob so we can slip inside the bathroom. I pause only for a second to catch my breath and look around. We're in the ladies' room.

I lock the door and pull Olivia back to me, reaching down to drag my hands up the backs of her legs, bringing her skirt up as I go.

Her panties leave the majority of her butt uncovered. I stroke the smooth skin with my palms, running my fingers along the crease between her cheeks, then pulling her hips snugly against mine. I want her to feel what she does to me.

She's panting into my mouth, and her fingers start fumbling with my belt buckle.

Damn, why did I wear a belt?

I help her get my jeans undone. I'm just about to reach inside them when she pushes my hand aside, wrapping her fingers around me and squeezing. I just about explode when she strokes me all the way to the tip and back down again, her tongue licking against mine in the same slow movement.

I grab her wrist and stop her. Olivia looks up at me with passion-dark eyes and a flushed face. Her lips are red and swollen and my only thought is of them wrapped around me, sucking me.

But not tonight. Tonight is all about Olivia—beautiful, sexy, courageous, passionate Olivia. Tonight, I want her to see what I see.

I turn her toward the sink, toward the only mirror in the room. She looks confused when she meets my eyes in the reflection.

"Look at yourself," I say. I pull her long hair over one shoulder and place a kiss in the bend of her neck. She tilts her head to give me better access. "You're the most beautiful girl in the bar." I run my hands across the exposed part of her stomach and up under her shirt. Her nipples are hard against my palms. I pinch them through the thin material of her bra, never taking my eyes off hers. Her lips part and she moans. "So sexy," I say, kneading her breasts, grinding my hips against the round globes of her ass.

I take one hand and move it down her stomach. Her skirt is still hiked up and I can see the white material of her panties. I run my fingers between her legs. I groan when I realize the soft cotton is soaked.

"Any man would die to have this for even one night," I say, pushing the material to the side and sliding my finger inside her. She closes her eyes and leans her head back against my shoulder. "No, I want you to watch. I want you to see what I see. I want us both to watch you come for me."

Obediently, she opens her eyes, her hips moving against my hand, her lips parted deliciously. I lean slightly away from her and place my hand in the center of her back. Gently I apply pressure until she bends forward, instinctively putting her hands on either edge of the sink to brace herself.

Still watching her, I curl my fingers in the elastic of her panties and I pull them down to her knees. Caressing one smooth ass cheek, I stick a finger from my other hand in my mouth then run it down between her legs, pushing it deep inside her. She moans and I feel her hot body squeeze me.

Taking her by the hips, I hold her still as I guide my tip into her. I bite back a moan at how hot and wet she feels, how her body sucks at me, pulling me farther in.

Her eyes are shifted downward, as if she'd like to watch me slide into her. When I don't move, hers eyes return to mine in the mirror. I nod and see them shift to her own reflection. And then I thrust into her, hard and deep.

Her mouth drops open and her eyes flutter shut in pleasure. I rest inside her, reveling in how tight she is, pausing so I don't come too fast.

She opens her eyes and leans forward, causing me to slide out of her almost completely. Then, just as slowly, she leans back, taking me fully inside her.

With my hands gripping her hips, I urge her into a slow tempo that I can sustain without getting off too soon. When she finds her rhythm, I reach around to slide my fingers between her slick folds, my fingertip moving easily over the hard nub there. She starts to make sexy little noises as I make small circles over her. She practically purrs when I find the spot she likes best.

After only a couple of minutes, I feel her body tightening around me. I know she's getting close. I increase my pace and tease her more insistently with my finger. When her breathing becomes more erratic and her pleasure becomes more vocal, I lean forward and fist my free hand in her hair, gently tipping her head back.

I speak into her ear. "I want you to watch yourself come all over me, Olivia. See how beautiful and sexy you are. See why I want you so much."

Relentlessly, I drive her up and up and up until she cries out, biting her lip to keep quiet, her sweet body racked with wave after wave of her orgasm.

I thrust into her until I can't take it anymore. I feel my own climax coming and I meet her eyes once more in the mirror. I can barely breathe past my racing heart. "See what you do to me? I want your eyes on mine when my come is running down your legs."

My words turn her on. I feel her spasm around me, squeezing me tight and pushing me over the edge. With a groan, I feel my every muscle stiffen as I shoot come deep inside her.

Although my instinct is to close them, I force my eyes to stay open, to remain trained on hers. She doesn't look away. Not for one second.

As I move slowly in and out of her in the aftermath, I feel warm liquid squeezing out around me, soaking the tops of my thighs. I'm sure she can feel it, too.

I grind my hips into her and she smiles.

Yeah, you can feel that, can't you, baby? And better yet, you like it.

My best discovery of the night? Olivia is hiding a dirty girl beneath that shy, quietly sexy exterior.

And I'm going to set her free.

TWENTY-FIVE

Olivia

Cash can't keep his hands off me as I try to put myself back together and exit the bathroom. I know I should be worried or embarrassed, and tomorrow I probably will be. But right now, I'm in awe. I've never had such a mind-blowing, body-rocking sexual experience in all my life.

On the one hand, I think it must've been Nash that came to my room. Based on this time with Cash . . . holy shit! But then again, Cash didn't ask about my birth control situation tonight, which makes me think he already knew. And that would mean it was him that came to my room.

But I have to keep in mind that something impulsive like this is probably very much in character for Cash. A guy like him probably assumes if I don't speak up, I've got birth control taken care of.

Once again, my revelation only leaves me with more questions. But at the moment, I don't care. I'm consumed by Cash. I still feel his touch. I still smell his scent. I still . . . feel him and it's a feeling I hope never goes away. I can't get him out of my head and, for right now, I'm okay with that.

I'm straightening my hair for the second time while Cash stands behind me, rubbing my bare stomach. My panties are still damp and, at this rate, they'll never be dry.

He smooths my hair, then pulls it away from my neck and starts nibbling. "Do we have to go back out there?"

I can't help but giggle. "I'm sure there are people who will need to use the restroom before the night's out."

"Screw 'em. There's another one."

I laugh outright. "Where are you staying?"

He looks up and meets my eyes in the mirror.

"I'll find a hotel somewhere. Why? You wanna come visit me?"

Um, hell yes!

I think that, but I don't say it. Rather, I turn around in his arms. "Look, you came all the way out here to help me. The least I can do is give you a place to stay. But my dad will be there, so . . ."

"So we have to be quiet," he whispers, waggling his eyebrows comically.

I just smile. I neither confirm nor deny that there will be more sex. But there will be. If he tries even a little, there definitely will be.

Slowly, we make our way to the door. I take a deep breath and flip open the lock.

"You go first. I'll wait a few minutes. That way it won't be *too* obvious," he says considerately.

I grin. "Um, I'm sure there will be very little doubt, but that's sweet of you to do, anyway."

I turn to pull open the door, but Cash puts his hand against it. When I look back, his lips crush mine in a fiery kiss that has me rethinking his suggestion that we stay in the bathroom.

But, alas, we can't.

The rest of the night proves to be one of the best I've spent in a long, long time. Cash stays close to me, always touching me in some small way, setting my skin on fire. We share lots of knowing smiles and glances that keep the moments in the bathroom fresh in my mind. Not that they wouldn't be otherwise. I'm pretty sure they'll still be fresh in my mind when I'm a hundred and nine and can't remember where I put my teeth. But there will always be Cash . . . in the bathroom . . . in the mirror . . .

Neither of us drinks much more. I think we're both content to keep our wits about us and not ruin the magic of the night. When everyone is all partied out, Cash walks me to Ginger's car so I can drive her home. I'm more than sober now. And happily so.

"I'll follow you so I can drive you back home."

"Okay," I agree with a wide smile. I can't seem to stop smiling.

He gives me a quick peck on the lips and then we part ways. All the way to Ginger's house, I find myself looking in the rearview mirror at the single headlight behind me.

And smiling. Of course, smiling.

"Well, I guess we know which one you pick, Liv," Ginger slurs from the passenger seat. I jump. We're almost to her house and this is the first time she's spoken. I thought she was passed out.

"Why do you say that?"

"Because he's a bad boy. And we both know you always pick the bad boy."

Her head slumps to the side after she deals me this blow.

I *do* always pick the bad boy. And I *do* always live to regret it. Am I making a huge mistake with Cash?

Her words haunt me from the time I drop her off to the time I walk Cash to his room after our trip home on the motorcycle. I leave him for the night after a very chaste kiss.

He stops me with a hand to my shoulder. "What's wrong?" he whispers. I'm sure he's curious why I'm going to bed without . . . him. He saw my father fast asleep on his bed downstairs.

I try to put some heart into my smile, but I imagine that I fail miserably. "Nothing. I'll see you in the morning. Sleep well."

I go to my own room, closing the door snugly behind me and then getting ready for bed. After more than an hour has passed and I'm still not asleep, I decide to take a shower, hoping it will refresh and relax me. Maybe it's the grime of the bar that's keeping me awake.

I'm standing beneath the hot spray of water, trying not to think too much, when I hear the metal curtain rings slide along the shower rod. I wipe my eyes and look up to see Cash stepping into the shower.

I can't help but go a little ga-ga over his naked body. It's even more perfect than I could've imagined. His chest is wide and tan and flawless but for the tattoo on his left pectoral. His stomach is flat and rippling with muscles. His legs are long and strong. Not one inch of him disappoints, including the several hard, proud, impressive ones that make my insides quiver.

I know I'm staring, but I can't help it. Just the sight of him makes me wet and ready.

A finger beneath my chin tilts my face up. Cash's expression is serious and sweet, his face devastatingly handsome.

"You worry too much. Can't you just trust me?"

His eyes are boring holes into mine. I want him so much, but I just don't know that giving in to him is the smart thing to do.

If only he were more like Nash . . .

"I don't know," I answer him honestly.

He nods in acceptance. "You'll learn to. I promise."

And then he kisses me. It's a slow, deep kiss that carries meaning and emotion, neither of which I know how to interpret.

I pull away to speak, but he puts his finger over my lips. "Shhh, just let me love you, okay? Don't think. Just feel."

His sinfully dark eyes are fathomless, but earnest. After several seconds, I nod. He smiles, then kisses me again. Tenderly.

With his lips and his tongue, he licks the water from my skin—from my neck, from my nipples, from my stomach. He kneels between my legs and brings me to the brink of ecstasy twice, stopping both times as if he's waiting for something.

When I'm nearly ready to explode a third time, he stands and kisses me again, grabbing the tops of my thighs and picking me up to press me against the shower wall. He lowers me onto his shaft, his tongue thrusting into my mouth, mimicking the movements of his body.

We climax together. He swallows my moans, no doubt in deference to my sleeping father. When we're done, and he's still buried inside me, he turns with me in his arms and holds me beneath the shower spray. The warm, massaging fingers of the water soothe me. I nearly fall asleep with my head on his shoulder.

Letting me down, Cash turns off the water and grabs the towel I laid out for myself. He dries me from head to toe and then carries me to the next room and puts me to bed, naked.

"Go to sleep," he says softly. "Don't think anymore. I'll see you in the morning."

And then he's gone.

And I go to sleep.

TWENTY-SIX

Cash

I wake up with a raging hard-on and only one girl on my mind. I can barely see the light of dawn coming through the curtains. I know I shouldn't wake her, but I'm almost afraid not to. As much as she gets caught up in her own head, it's hard to tell what mindset she'll be in when she wakes up.

So I go to her.

I open the door a crack and listen. I can hear her father snoring downstairs, so I slip out of my room and down the hall, silently entering Olivia's room.

I move quietly. I'm relieved that her breathing remains deep and even. She's lying on her side, facing away from me. Stripping off my jeans, I peel back the covers just enough to slide beneath them. I ease in beside her and snuggle up close to her back.

In her sleep, she wiggles her butt against me, settling in closer. I bite my lip to keep from making any noise. She's still naked and the crease of her ass is teasing me.

I reach around and cup one of her perfect breasts. Even in sleep, her body responds to me, the nipple puckering. I pinch it lightly between my fingertips and she moans a little, pushing her ass into me again. This time, I push back, grinding my hips against hers.

I lean forward and kiss her neck, letting my hand trail down her flat stomach to the little thatch of neatly trimmed hair covering what I want most. Obligingly, she shifts, parting her legs enough for me to slide a finger between her folds. I rub her slowly, gently, until I feel her hips move with the rhythm of my hand.

Easing a finger inside her, I find that she's already dripping wet. My body jumps in anticipation, flexing against her backside.

I move my hand down to cup her thigh and bring her leg up onto my top one. It opens her enough that I can guide myself into her from behind. It's all I can do not to groan loudly when I slip into her tight sheath. I inhale deeply so as not to make any noise. She tips her hips back toward me, giving me an even deeper penetration. I don't know if it's intentional or instinctive. I still can't be sure if she's awake.

Working my fingers back to her moist center, I rub her toward orgasm as I move slowly in and out of her wet heat. When I feel her muscles begin to clench around me, her hand comes up to my hip, gripping me, pulling me tighter against her.

She's awake.

I hear her breathing pick up and then she gasps. I feel the spasms of her orgasm and hear her panting softly. I hold her firm and steady as I drive into her, harder and harder.

And then an explosion of sensation and I'm coming inside her. Before I even realize it, my teeth are biting into her shoulder. It seems to stir her. She brings her hand up and fists her fingers in my hair, pulling it a little, making me jerk inside her.

Damn, I can't wait to see what she's like when she lets go.

TWENTY-SEVEN

Olivia

I can't stop smiling. Again. Even though doubt niggles at the back of my mind, it's impossible to think entirely bad thoughts when I'm lying on Cash's chest, tracing his tattoo.

"What does this mean?" I whisper.

"It's the Chinese symbol for awesome," he teases lightly.

I giggle. "If it's not, which I imagine it isn't, then it should be."

"Are you paying me a compliment? I just want to be sure, so I don't miss it."

I slap his ribs. "You make it sound like I'm mean and horrible because I don't throw myself at your feet."

"You don't have to throw yourself at my feet. Although if you want to, I'm sure I can think of something for you to do while you're down there."

I look up at him and he's waggling his eyebrows again.

"I'm sure you could." Shaking my head, I settle back onto his chest and resume tracing the ink shapes. "Seriously, what do they mean?"

Cash is quiet for so long I begin to think he's not going to answer me. But then he finally speaks.

"It's a collage of things that remind me of my family."

I look at each line, not really able to see any discernible images. I trace the things that look like dark fingers. "And these?"

"They symbolize the fire that took them from me."

I lean up onto my elbow and look down into his face.

"What do you mean?"

He looks disconcerted for a second before he answers. "Well, my mother was killed in a boating explosion that was intended for my entire family. My father is in prison for her murder. My brother and I are very . . . separated. In all the ways that matter, that fire took my family. My home. Now, it's just me."

I think back to Nash telling me about his father being in prison for murder. We never got to talk more about it, so I didn't know his mother was dead and his father was to blame.

I want to know more, of course. I have a thousand questions, but I don't want to push.

"Do you . . . feel like talking about it?"

His smile is polite and sad. "Not really. If you don't mind. I hate to ruin a day that has started out this perfectly." His grin widens when he reaches down to cup my butt. I feel him getting hard against my belly where I'm half lying on him.

I grin, too. "Well, you're just gonna have to cool your jets.

My dad will be up soon and I may not have mentioned that he's a crack shot with a pistol."

"In that case, how about breakfast instead?"

I giggle. "Wise choice, braveheart."

"Don't tease. How much good would I be to you if I let your dad blow my dick off?"

I say nothing, only smile. But inside, I feel my heart plummet. Already I'm thinking that there's so much more to Cash than the fact that he's great between the sheets. He's charming and witty, he's considerate and passionate. He's smart and resourceful. He's all sorts of wonderful things that have nothing to do with his prowess in the bedroom.

And in a public bathroom. And against the shower wall.

Those thoughts have me feeling lighthearted again in no time.

After Cash sneaks back to his bedroom, I head for the shower. Again. I need to actually bathe this time.

I smile the entire time. There's not a place on my body that doesn't seem to be marked with Cash as I rub over it with the soap. And it's a decidedly nice feeling. For the moment, anyway.

The reality of my situation threatens to intrude once more. And once more, I brush it back. Ruthlessly. Relentlessly. I'll deal with it on Monday. But I'm taking this weekend and calling a time out. Time out from wisdom and responsibility and all the voices in my head. This weekend is only about Cash and me and all the mad attraction between us.

After dressing in cut-off jean shorts and a *Boys Over Books* T-shirt, I head downstairs. I'm a little surprised by what I find.

My father is sitting at the kitchen table. His casted leg is propped up on a stool, his crutches are against the wall behind him, and there's a day's growth of stubble in place. The most surprising thing, however, is that he's chatting up a storm with Cash, who appears to be making breakfast.

A thousand different feelings bubble in my chest as I watch the scene. Not one of them is welcome. Each of them means trouble for me. And for my heart.

If only you were more like Nash, I think as I watch Cash add spices to beaten eggs as my father directs him.

"Good morning," I say brightly, trying to hide the sinking feeling that's dragging my heart into a pit of despair.

They both turn to greet me with light and happy smiles. Cash winks at me from in front of the stove, and pure lust twitches in my lower belly. There's no denying this man is hot. Effing hot. Probably hotter than the stove he's cooking on.

I jump in to help and let myself fall into a morning that is nothing short of surreal in its Rockwellian charm and appeal. As I sit scarfing down eggs, bacon, pancakes, and coffee, I know that every other morning for the rest of my life will be measured against this one. And probably come up wanting. By an enormous margin.

Dammit.

After cleaning up the breakfast dishes, Cash helps get Dad settled back into his chair and we head for the barn. On the way, Cash peppers me with questions about raising sheep and what all it entails. I try to answer them as quickly and as succinctly as I can, although it's hard to cram a lifetime of knowledge and experience into a few short minutes.

"So what is it we're doing today, then?"

"We are going out to look for the new lambs. The ewes separate themselves and have their babies out in the woods or field. We need to make sure the lambs are healthy, though, and not having any problems that we need to treat. I'll record them and which ewe they belong to. That way, too, we know roughly how long to wait to bring them in to tag them, dock the female tails, and band the male testicles."

"Dock their tails? Band their testicles? Why?" Cash asks, looking fairly horrified at such a barbaric notion.

"We dock the female tails because it's much easier and cleaner for the ewes when they give birth. It's for the safety of both the mother and her offspring. Plus, it's also a way to tell them apart from the young males.

"As for the males, we neuter them because . . . well, you know what they'd do if we didn't."

Once his shock over the procedure wears off, he grins and waggles his eyebrows. "Yeah, I do!"

Smiling at him, I throw my leg over the wide, padded seat of the four-wheeler and pat the spot behind me. "Now, it's my turn to drive," I inform him in my wickedest voice.

Cash cocks one eyebrow in that way that I love and very slowly slides onto the seat behind me. He scoots in close, grabbing my hips and pulling me snugly into the V of his legs, pressing his chest to my back. I can feel him along every inch of my posterior. He winds his arms around my waist, his hands settling perversely low on my stomach, making my insides twitch with desire.

I feel his lips against my ear when he whispers, "Ready when you are."

With shaking fingers, I turn the key and crank the ignition. When I rev the engine, I figure there's no way it's running with more RPMs than my libido is at this very moment. If Cash doesn't cool it, I'll be sitting in a puddle within the hour.

I pull out of the barn and stop shortly after to open the first gate. One of our several herding dogs runs out to meet us. I reach down to pet his enormous white head. "Solomon! How are you boy?" I ask of the Great Pyrenees.

I bend down and he licks my cheek vigorously, then moves back so I can push the gate wide and pull the four-wheeler through. Cash gets off to close the gate behind us, and that becomes our routine through each gate of each field of the vast 170-acre farm of my childhood.

I drive us up and down and around the old familiar paths of my youth, pointing out along the way places and things I think Cash might find interesting. He asks several relevant and insightful questions, leaving me in no doubt that his intellectual aptitude is at least equal to Nash's.

Smart and *hot*. *Dammit.*

Cash helps me look for ewes with new lambs. He points out several that are from the spring. Not having been around them his whole life, he can't look at them and see the subtle differences that indicate they are older. But I see it immediately.

In the end, we find seven late-season lambs. They're a result of Rambo, one of our rams, escaping his pen again and finding his way to the ewes. Normally, Dad tries to keep all the mating in certain months so that the ewes have the lambs in spring. But occasionally, something like this happens and leaves him scrambling to account for surprise lambs.

I make note of each lamb we've spotted. According to my father, he was expecting to find seven to nine. What this tells me is either we'll find a couple more tomorrow when we come out or we'll find a couple dead somewhere.

Even after all these years, my heart squeezes at the thought. There's nothing worse than losing lambs.

On the way back toward the front field, we see two other dogs and Pedro, the llama. Of course Cash makes a comment about each. I can't help but laugh at his witty observations.

My lighthearted attitude toward the day concerns me, though. Despite the danger of it, I can feel myself being pulled in by Cash, *to* Cash. It's like looking out on the horizon and seeing a whole new realm of feeling lying just ahead. Along with the ominous clouds of a storm. It would be all too easy for me to imagine us one day taking over the farm. Together.

And thinking like that would be a disaster.

Rather than going all the way back to the house, I drive us to the north barn. Playing with Solomon at every stop is a dirty business, because he's filthy. Plus, riding through the tall grass flings all sorts of bugs and debris, essentially adding another layer of dirt on top of the first one.

So I head to the barn so we can clean up. It's the closest place with running water.

I let Cash clean up first. Then, after I've washed my hands

and arms, I wet a paper towel to wipe off with. I drag it over my sweaty neck and chest, then up my arms as well.

When I'm finished, I move to throw it in the trash and find Cash watching me. He's leaned up against the wall with his arms crossed over his chest, staring. He's not smiling, but there's a look on his face I'm becoming familiar with. A heat in his eyes. It's dark and dangerous, and it has the ability to burn me up if I'm not careful.

I stop. Not on purpose, but because I feel the world shift beneath my feet when he unfolds his body and moves slowly toward me. I feel like I've been chosen by a lion as his mate and he's stalking me.

Cash stops in front of me. He doesn't say a word. He just bends and scoops me up into his arms and carries me back to the four-wheeler.

I parked it in the sun on the crest of a hill. It's obscured by woods on three sides. The only thing in the field below is grass. No people, no eyes. Just grass. Tall, tall grass, swaying calmly in the warm breeze.

He climbs onto the four-wheeler and sets me in his lap. He looks into my eyes for several intense seconds, watching me like I'm all he sees. And he's all I see. For this moment, it seems we are completely alone in the world, each wholly consumed by the other. Nothing else exists.

It scares me that I like it that way. Just him and me. Nobody else.

Cupping my face, Cash kisses me. It's not an overtly ravenous kiss, but there's something just beneath the surface that scorches my insides. It's as though he's trying to absorb something from my soul, like he's taking more than just the physical.

With practiced hands, he unbuttons my shorts and rubs his palm across my naked belly. Chills spread down my legs and heat pools in my core. A volcano of hot lava seems always to be boiling just under my skin whenever Cash is around.

Winding an arm around me, Cash lifts me and pushes my shorts and my panties down my legs, then tucks them behind the seat. Still, he hasn't spoken. And still, there is that implied danger in being with him, in letting him take me where he wants to go.

But I go. I have to. I'm helpless against it. At least for today. Maybe not tomorrow. But today, I go.

Never taking his eyes off mine, Cash scoots back a little and unzips his pants. I can't help but look down and revel in the absolute perfection of him.

With confident fingers, I reach out and grip his thick shaft, stroking the hard satin length. When I hear him groan, I see one glistening drop of liquid appear on the head. Sliding back on the seat, I bend forward and touch my tongue to the tip, licking the drop. Then licking him again.

I close my lips around him and feel Cash's fingers fist in my hair. I can't fit much of him into my mouth, so I lick and suck my way up and down the sides, cupping his balls and teasing them with my lips and tongue.

Then Cash is pulling me up, kissing me. Thrusting his tongue into my mouth, tasting himself in my saliva. Roughly, he grabs my hips and lifts until I'm straddling him. Then, in one sharp movement, he flexes his hips and pulls me down onto him, impaling me.

I can't stop the cry of pleasure that escapes my lips. It feels as though it's torn from somewhere deep. Against my will.

I ride Cash in the bright sunlight, both of us gasping in the fresh air. I moan when he nibbles my ear. I whimper when he lifts my shirt and bites my nipple through my bra. He tells me how it feels to be inside me. He whispers things he dreams of doing to me.

I don't need Cash to tell me I'm all he's thinking of, that I'm all that's on his mind. I can see it in his face, feel it in his kiss. For now, he's all mine. And I'm all his.

Absorbed by his passion, by his eyes, by his touch, I lose my grasp on reality when my body succumbs to the throes of my orgasm. The only thing I'm aware of is Cash's breath in my ear and the feel of him coming in time with me. With each pulse, I feel heat shooting into me, intensifying my own pleasure.

I'm breathless, my arms and legs wrapped tight around Cash. He's panting against the skin of my throat, his hands splayed over my back, hugging me to him.

I could stay this way forever.

If only Cash were the forever type.

His arms tighten around me as if he knows what I'm thinking. I sigh into his neck and hope that he doesn't.

TWENTY-EIGHT

Cash

The drive from Salt Springs to Atlanta Sunday night isn't exactly a luxurious one. I mean, we're on the back of a motorcycle. But still, Olivia seems comfortable. I feel her rest her cheek against my back. Her thighs are pressed tight against mine and she's snuggled up like she's content.

Only I get the feeling she's not. She's stuck on something in her head again, and I don't know what to do about it.

We had sex a dozen times over the weekend, and all I can think about is the next time, the next thing I want to do with her, for her, to her. I can't seem to get enough of her.

But it bugs the shit out of me that each time feels like the last time with her. Like she's holding something back. I can feel it. I can see it in her eyes sometimes when she's taken off guard. When she doesn't have enough time to hide it behind a smile. Something's bothering her. I think I know what it is. But I'm just not sure I can fix it, that I'm *capable* of fixing it.

When I pull up in front of her place, I push the bike onto the kickstand but I don't cut the engine. Something tells me she's not going to invite me in.

And she doesn't.

"I can't thank you enough for everything you've done this weekend."

She's *thanking* me?

I smile, my normal carefree smile. "Oh, believe me, it was my pleasure."

She smiles, too, but it's tinged with sadness. And maybe inevitability. I think, in her mind, we were over before we even got started. The question is whether I can change her mind. And how.

Even *I* notice the uncomfortable silence, and I *never* notice them. Very little bothers me. But this does.

I need time to think. But I need to make sure she *doesn't*. That's when I get into trouble. At least in her head, I do.

"So, you said you could look over some stuff at the club this week, not on your regular shifts. How about tomorrow evening? You don't have to stay late."

I can tell I've thwarted her. She was probably already think-ing of ways she could avoid me. But that's not going to happen. I'll get past whatever is bothering her. I won't give her a choice in the matter.

"I'll take that as a yes. And by then you'll have your car back. I'll bring it by early in the morning."

Watching her expression is like watching a pile-on with a bunch of kids. And she's the person on the bottom, about to run out of air. I know I should feel guilty for making her feel that way, but I don't. Not really. I know she'd get some crazy idea in her head that I'm bad for her. And that's just not true. In fact, the longer I know her, the more time I spend with her, the more I believe I'm exactly what she needs in her life. She just doesn't know it yet. But she will. I'll have to tell her the truth eventually. But I'll wait as long as I can. It could be a disaster otherwise.

Finally she nods. "Okay. Sounds good. And thank you. Again. Cash, I don't know—"

"Hey, don't worry about it. Maybe now you'll see I'm not all bad."

I know she's getting ready to respond to that, so I kiss her partially open mouth, slip on my helmet, and take off down the road.

The best thing I can do is keep that girl's mind—and her mouth—busy.

This ought to be fun.

TWENTY-NINE

Olivia

What the hell am I gonna do?

I collapse onto my bed, facedown. I realize I'm in serious trouble. Cash is not the kind of guy I can let myself fall for.

I don't think I really thought I'd get this involved with him. Not really. I mean, he's sexy and flirty and fun and flattering, but I never imagined that if we managed to actually have sex it would turn so quickly into . . . this. Whatever *this* is.

It was a huge mistake to spend so much time with him at home. With my father. At the one place on earth that's like my sanctuary. Putting him there, in that context, and him being so sweet and fitting in so perfectly, just made me fall into all sorts of traps and clichés.

Dammit.

As if my mother has taken over a large portion of my brain, I find myself ticking off all the negatives of Cash and all the positives of Nash, pitting them against each other in a death match.

I wish I could shut out her voice in my head, telling me it will never work with Cash, that he's not what I need. I can practically hear her gushing about how perfect Nash is.

And she's right.

The fact that he wants me gives me hope. The fact that he's taken is quickly being outweighed by the fact that he fights it, by the fact that he's trying to do the right thing by Marissa. Even if she is a cold, nasty snake of a girl.

I know I'm not thinking clearly. I'm in Defcon 5 mode, brought on by sheer panic over my feelings for Cash. But no matter how hard I try, I can't pull out of the tailspin. My mother's voice is too strong, her claws too deep. And seeing Gabe over the weekend isn't helping.

It's the perfect anti-Cash storm. And it's wreaking havoc.

Before I can even think twice, I'm dialing Nash's number. Maybe I can put his side of things to rest once and for all. One way or the other. Either there's a chance or there's not, but I can't keep holding him up as the other viable option if he isn't.

At first, I'm a little relieved when he doesn't answer. But then, when he finally does, I'm more relieved to hear his voice.

"Nash, it's Olivia. I'm sorry to bother you so late. Were you busy?"

"Uh, no. I'm just getting in. Is everything all right?"

Where do I begin? I don't even know what to say now that I've got him.

"Yes, everything's fine." I pause to collect my scattered

thoughts. "Actually, no it's not. Is there any way you could come over?"

"Over there? Tonight?"

Something in his voice—some note of hesitation—nearly shakes me out of my frenzy. Nearly, but not quite. I ignore it and move on.

"Yes. Tonight. As soon as you can."

"What's the matter, Olivia? You're starting to scare me. Has something happened? Did my brother do something to you?"

I hear an edge to his voice and I'm confused by it. It takes me a full three or four seconds to figure out what he's getting at. "What? Cash? No. Oh, God, no! It's nothing like that at all."

Why would he even ask that? Does he really feel that way about his own flesh and blood?

I hear him exhale. "Okay, good. I'll be there in about twenty minutes."

"Great. Thanks. See you then."

I wait. And, as I wait, I pace. And not-so-patiently, I might add. I'm teetering between two horrible options—being bold with Nash or moving to Siberia.

By the time I hear the doorbell, Siberia is looking pretty dang good.

I fling open the door, completely unprepared for Nash like this. He must've been working late. He's wearing a black suit that fits him to perfection. His bright red tie is askew and his hair is mussed, making him look even more like Cash. He's like dream Cash. Cash with a little more Nash.

Why can't they both be a little more like each other?

I answer that thought.

Because then you'd want them both. Just like you do now. Only without any reasons to stay away.

Shaking my head, I step back to allow him to pass. He walks lazily to the couch and flops down, like he's tired. I perch on the other end of the sofa, facing him.

"Rough day?"

He wags his head back and forth. "Meh, some parts."

I swallow hard. "I'm sorry to call so late."

"It's not a problem. I was still up. Besides, I told you to call if you needed anything."

I stare at him, at the face that seems so familiar to me now. It feels odd for it to be attached to Nash's personality, though. To not feel the intense heat of Cash emanating from behind those sparkling midnight eyes.

He raises his eyebrows in question when I don't speak. "So, what's up?"

I might never know what came over me. One second I'm wondering what the hell I'm doing. The next I'm blurting out embarrassing-isms.

"Nash, do you want me?"

If I weren't so shocked at what just came out of my mouth, I'd probably think his expression was comical. As it is, I'm dying a little on the inside.

"What?"

I scoot closer to him, laying my hand on his arm for emphasis. "Do you want me?"

"I think we've already established the answer to that. What's this about, Olivia?"

I'm floundering. I'll admit it. And my go-to plan was never even a forethought, much less a plan. So I wing it. Which, in this case, translates to practically assaulting Nash.

Leaning forward, I press my lips to his. I don't know who is the more shocked of us, Nash or me. At first, his lips are frozen beneath mine. If possible, I think my humiliation rises. But then, he jerks back like he's been burned.

Nash grabs me by the upper arms, his fingers digging into the tender flesh, and he looks me square in the eye. For a few seconds, I could swear I see hurt and anger. However, that makes no sense. But then, when I blink, it's gone, making me wonder if I'd imagined it altogether.

His lips curve into a cruel twist. "So this is how it is," he says enigmatically. I try to pull out of his grasp; his fingers are really starting to hurt. But he won't let go. Pulling me into his lap, he roughly cups my face. "Is this what you want?"

Before I can answer, his lips are crushing mine. They're not gentle. They're not passionate. They're not even sexual. They're punishing and angry and . . . cold.

I'm cringing away from him when his tongue forces its way past my lips. His mouth is mashed so tightly to mine, for a second I think I taste blood. Then the flavor is mingled with something salty. It's then I realize I'm crying.

Nash pulls away from me, opening his mouth as if to curse me, but he stops in shock. I guess he sees that I'm crying and the Nash I thought I knew takes over.

His face softens and, tenderly, he raises one hand and wipes the tears from my left cheek. I feel my chin tremble. I will it to stay still, but the damn thing completely ignores me.

"Did I hurt you?" he whispers, scattering tiny butterfly kisses all over my lips and cheeks. "I'm so sorry, baby."

"I'm sorry," I whisper. "I shouldn't have done that. I know you're with Marissa. I don't know what came over me."

Nash leans back and looks at me. "Am I what you want?"

I don't know what to say to that. Should I admit that I do? Am I even sure that I still feel that way?

Cash drifts through my mind.

As if sensing the direction my thoughts have taken, Nash asks, "What about my brother? I thought . . . I mean, I know he spent the weekend in Salt Springs."

I'd forgotten that Cash had to get directions from Nash. If possible, I'm even more humiliated. No doubt he thinks I'm a huge whore now.

Before I can respond, Nash continues. "Or was I there, too?" He brushes his lips over mine. "Did you think of my lips when he kissed you?" Light as a feather, he runs his hand down the outside of my thigh and back up again, squeezing my hip. "Did you wish it were me touching you? Like I did the night I came to your room?"

I gasp in shock.

Ohmigod! It was Nash!

I start to lean back and speak, but his lips take mine, quickly coaxing them apart. Sensation drowns out thought as I feel him breathe into my mouth. "Do you still want me? Because if you do, I'm all yours." With that, he deepens the kiss, his tongue licking along mine, his free hand roaming across my waist and stomach. Chills spread over me. His touch is so much like Cash's.

Cash . . .

I push against Nash's chest. He moves back easily, giving me no resistance.

He looks down into my eyes. Neither of us says a word.

He nods and his lips curve into a smile of acceptance rather than humor.

"Good night, Olivia."

He doesn't move right away. He just watches me.

Eventually, I nod and slide off his lap, coming to my feet. I walk him to the door and he pulls it open. He turns as if to say something else, but changes his mind. I watch as he disappears into the darkness, not once looking back at me.

It's no wonder I get virtually no sleep. Between finding out that I've slept with Nash, feeling worse and worse about making a complete and utter fool of myself with him last night, and the predicament I now find myself in, I blow off my Monday classes and head to Cash's instead. I'm not sure why I feel the need to go to him; maybe it's a sense that I've somehow betrayed him. I don't know. But I find myself drawn to him for some reason. And I don't question it. I just go.

I know he's at least awake, because I saw my car parked at

the curb when I looked out the window this morning. My keys were in an envelope in the mailbox.

The first time I came to Dual during the day, Cash was expecting me, so the front door was unlocked. I wondered if that was the case all the time.

Evidently not, I think as I pull on both doors to find them both secured. And I didn't get a key with my employment because Cash always opens and closes. I mean, why wouldn't he? He lives behind the bar, for Pete's sake.

I walk around the side of the building. I'm pretty sure there is at least a back door, some way to take out garbage and for Cash to get in and out from wherever he parks that motorcycle of his.

One side of the building has no door, so I continue on around. As I suspected, there is a door at the back. It empties out into the alley where there is a huge trash Dumpster against the opposite wall. Unfortunately, the back door is locked, too.

I keep walking, around to the other side of the building, hoping for another door. And I hit pay dirt. There's a side door. A big one.

It looks like Cash has converted a back corner of the club into an apartment and garage. I can tell by the nature of the wide, roll-up bay-type door. That and the fact that it's open and his bike is parked inside. That's kind of a dead giveaway.

I'm a little confused, however, when I see Nash's car parked inside as well. Or at least it's a vehicle that *looks* like Nash's car.

My stomach twists into a nervous knot. I know they're not

exactly close, but that doesn't mean they wouldn't discuss me. I mean, they very much have me in common! Even more so after recent events.

I feel a little nauseated. I'm debating scampering back to my car when the interior door opens and Cash walks out. He doesn't see me as he turns immediately to lock the door behind him. He's also on the phone, which he tucks against his shoulder as he sets the deadbolt.

I can't help but overhear his end of the conversation.

"Marissa, I told you I had meetings all weekend. There was just no way for me to do that. I didn't have—"

He stops dead when he turns and sees me standing at the edge of the door. I'm sure my mouth is hanging open and I probably look every bit as confused as I feel.

One question is running on a loop through my mind. *Why is Cash talking to Marissa that way? Why is Cash talking to Marissa that way?*

We stare at each other for the longest minute of my entire life. It is so quiet in the garage, I can actually hear Marissa repeating *Nash's* name over and over and over again.

Finally, without taking his eyes off mine, he addresses her. "I've gotta go. I'll call you later." And he hangs up.

He studies me for so long I begin to think he's not going to say anything to me at all. But then he does.

"Why don't you come in? We need to talk."

My heart is thudding against my ribs. Hard! I was expecting any number of logical explanations. Maybe he was playing a prank. Maybe he was covering something up for Nash.

Maybe I just misunderstood something. But the way Cash is watching me makes me think something is very, very wrong. And that I'm not going to like it.

I think of leaving. Of just walking right back to my car. These boys have been trouble for me from day one. If I were smart, I'd turn around and never look back.

But I know why I can't. Even as the thought runs through my head, the thought of never seeing Cash again cuts through my chest like a knife blade. I feel the pain of it, the devastation of it. The life-changing wound of it. I feel everything but the blood, the blood that should be soaking my clothes.

I nod once and walk slowly, numbly across the polished floor to where he's holding the now-open door for me.

I feel like I'm going to an execution.

Of my heart and my trust, maybe.

And that's pretty much right.

THIRTY

Cash

My pulse is racing. Just the thought of coming clean, of telling any one person all my secrets scares the shit out of me. I'm not sure why I'm going to tell Olivia. I just know that I am. That I have to. I have to trust her if I ever expect her to trust me. The thing is, I still haven't figured out why that matters so much to me. Why I even care.

But I do. A whole hell of a lot.

She knows something's up. She looks like she's walking the plank and there are sharks in the water. I guess, in a way, there are. If one could consider me and my family's history sharks.

I don't even really see the mess I left in my house last night. When I got back from Olivia's I shed my suit and left it crumpled on the floor right before I re-dressed as myself and went out to close up the club. Afterward, I'd fallen onto the bed, face first, and slept like the dead. Until Jake had come pounding at my door this morning, ready to deliver Olivia's car. This double life thing is for the birds!

And now here I am, getting ready to tell someone, a girl whom I haven't known very long at all, my deepest, darkest, dirtiest, most dangerous secret. And the only thing I'm worried about is whether she'll ever want to see me again. How's that for crazy?

"Do you want something to drink? I just turned the coffeepot off, so it's still hot."

She's looking around in a daze, no doubt trying to fit the pieces into the puzzle. But she won't. Never in a thousand years would she ever guess. Unless I tell her.

"Olivia, have a seat on the couch. I'll bring you some coffee. Then we'll talk."

I think she needs it more than I do, which is saying a lot. I pour us both a mug of coffee and run some hot water in the empty decanter, setting it back on the warmer until I can wash it out later. I've been taking care of myself for a long time. Some housekeeping things just come naturally at this point.

I hand her a cup and sit in the chair opposite her. I don't want to crowd her and make what I'm about to say any worse. She'll probably need a little space, a little distance after she hears it.

It surprises me when she speaks first. I don't know why it would, though. Her backbone is obviously pretty sturdy. She just doesn't always tap into it. But when she needs to, it's there.

Like now.

"I don't like games. I don't like lies. Just tell me what's going on. The truth."

Her face is set. She's braced herself. I guess if ever there's a good time to drop a bomb like this, now's probably it.

"All I ask is that you give me a chance to fully explain. Don't go running off without hearing the whole story. Deal?"

She doesn't agree immediately, which makes me a little nervous. But when she does, I know she means it.

"Deal."

I wonder for a second whether I should tell her that repeating what she's about to hear would be disastrous, but I decide against it. That's like implying right off the bat that I don't trust her, which I do. It's just that I've never trusted anybody—*anybody*—with this before. I'm sure it's natural to be a little leery.

"I'm Cash."

Olivia just stares at me for a few seconds. I can only imagine how her mind must be spinning.

"I know that," she says calmly. "But I want to know, why were you acting like Nash?"

"Because I'm Nash, too."

Her blank look says I just totally confused her, totally boggled her mind.

"What's that supposed to mean?"

I know she will never be able to fully fathom what's going on unless I explain it to her from the beginning.

Here goes.

"My father got mixed up with some pretty . . . unsavory

people when he was younger, trying to make some extra money to help support his family. They were very poor. But this was all before he met my mother." I laugh bitterly. "Turns out once you're connected with people like that, you can never truly escape. I think, on some level, he knew that. But he tried, anyway. And when he did, they decided to impress upon him what a bad idea it was to try to leave. These people make their points in truly . . . unforgettable ways. This time it was to tamper with Dad's boat."

Olivia is watching me closely, listening. I have no idea if she believes a word I'm saying, but I'm not stopping now. I'm going to tell her the whole story. Right now. No more secrets.

"We were going on a family vacation. Over Christmas break. Just a short trip, really. My mother and brother had gone down a little early to take some supplies. No one thought they'd be on the boat that soon. There was an explosion. They were both killed. And burned up in the fire."

Her face shows no sign of any kind of reaction for at least two full minutes. I don't say a word as she digests what I've told her so far. I can tell the instant it sinks in. Every bit of color drains from her face.

"Was your brother a twin? Was he really named Nash?"

"Yes."

I hear her exhale. The breath is shaky, as are her hands where she's picking at her fingernails.

"So there was a Nash, but I've never met him," she states calmly. Maybe a little too calmly.

"Correct."

"So all this time, you've been pretending to be your brother."

"Correct."

"Why?"

"The people my father was involved with had set up several things that would cast suspicion on him. They called him with a warning right before they blew up the boat. Told him if he ever tried to rat them out, they'd kill everyone he ever knew or loved. At the time, they didn't realize Mom and Nash were on the boat.

"We tried to get in touch with my mother but couldn't. By the time we got there, the boat was already in pieces all over the bay. Not only did we both have to deal with the murder of Mom and Nash, but we both knew he'd go to prison, at the very least for something like negligent homicide. And it would only add to the sentence if there were two deaths pinned on him. That's when I decided to be both of us. If Nash had survived, Dad would only be supposedly guilty of one murder. There wasn't much else I could do, but I thought I could pull that much off. And I did. I guess in a way we were lucky that only a few of my mother's remains survived the fire."

"And this was how long ago?"

"Seven years ago. December of my senior year of high school."

She looks suspicious. Incredulous, too, but mostly suspicious.

"And no one was the wiser? How is that even possible?"

I know my laugh is bitter. She'll enjoy this part.

"You were right about me. I was always the bad boy, the rebel. I dropped out of high school after my junior year. I wanted to run this club that my father had just bought, and I knew I didn't need a diploma for that."

She raises her eyebrows. "This club?"

I nod.

"Nash was always the clean-cut, jock, honor student type. He was going places and everybody in the family knew it. Hell, everybody who knew *him* knew it. They would never have suspected for one second that it was me coming to class in his place. Me making the grades. Me picking up his diploma. Me going off to college. No one expected much of anything from me. Well, nothing but a life of quasi crime, like my father. All I had to do was show up at a party occasionally and show my ass so people wouldn't forget that I was alive, too, and then the focus would go back to Nash. It was easy. People wanted to forget me."

I can't keep all the bitterness I've buried for so long from leaching out into my voice. It's almost like I want her to see it, want her to feel it. Like her knowing will somehow make it less painful. I don't know why that is, what it is about this girl that makes a difference, but instinctively I know it does. *She* does.

"So all this time, you've been leading two separate lives. Lying to everyone in the world. Including the police."

My stomach feels hollow at her words. "Yes."

Of all the pain I've endured, I think what actually hurts the most is the disgust I see on her face.

"Why? How? How could you do that? To the living, but also to the memory of the dead?"

I feel tired. So tired. Suddenly, the toll of this life and the deception of it feels like a freight train sitting on my chest.

"I lost everything in that explosion. Everyone I ever loved was taken from me. Everything I called home was gone in the blink of an eye. I thought the least I could do was bring some kind of honor to their memory."

"This is how you honor their memory?"

I squeeze the bridge of my nose, wishing I could curtail the increasing throb I feel behind my eyes. "It's kind of hard to explain. Both my parents wanted nothing more than for Nash and me to make something of ourselves. Anything would've been better than to follow in our father's footsteps. And Nash was brilliant. He had so much ahead of him. So much more than I did. It just didn't seem right that he would be the one to end up dead. I did the best I could to make my parents proud and to give Nash the name and the reputation that he deserved. That he would've had if he were alive."

Olivia is absolutely silent. That would worry me if not for the look of sympathetic understanding that I can see rising in her eyes, on her expressive face. As tender and good-hearted as she is, maybe she'll be able to understand my reasoning. I just have to make sure to explain it all to her. In depth.

"On top of that, I knew that if I pursued a law degree, there might be a chance I could do something to help my father."

She perks up at that. I'm not surprised at all that Olivia is the type to root for the underdog, to feel the need to find justice, that kind of thing. She's just a good person. Much better than I deserve. Nash would be worthy of her. But not me.

And yet I can't seem to make myself stay away from her.

"Do you really think you could change things? Make a difference?"

I shrug. "I don't know, but I'm certainly looking into it. It's one of the biggest reasons I wanted in with a big, powerful law firm, like your uncle's."

"Do they know?" she asks. "About your father, I mean?"

"Yes. That's not something I thought I could keep secret, so I've been honest with a few select people about it. And they know what I'm working toward, that I want to help him win an appeal. I've been able to get some incredible insight by observing some of the partners and being involved there."

Olivia nods but doesn't say anything for what seems like forever. But when she does, it is very much worth the wait.

She's looking down at her fingers, either because she doesn't want me to see that she cares or because she's still not sure she does. But I feel such profound relief, I don't need to see her eyes. Her words say it all.

"Is it dangerous?"

I smile. "No, I don't think so. My father has kept quiet all this time. I hope he's fallen off their radar."

"Kept quiet?"

I pause. And then there's this part. "Uh, yeah. He was, um,

pretty desperate to get away and he chose an . . . inadvisable way to try to regain his freedom."

"And what inadvisable way was that?"

I exhale loudly. "Blackmail."

Her mouth drops open in disbelief. "Your dad tried to blackmail the mob? Has he never seen *The Godfather*?"

I can't help but laugh. "I don't think that's quite like the reality of things, but yeah, it was pretty stupid. What he did." I feel that old familiar spike of pain radiate through my chest. "He paid dearly for his mistake. We all did."

"What was the blackmail? Or should I not ask things like that?"

She's curious, yes, but I can see by her face she's *cautiously* curious.

"He took a couple of books. Accounting books. Ledgers."

Olivia gasps and covers her mouth with both her hands. "Holy shit," I hear her say behind them. Her emerald eyes are wide with disbelief. "Ohmigod, it's just like the movies! Did he turn them over to anyone?"

I shake my head sharply. "No! That was part of their threat. If he were to give them to the police, we'd all be dead."

"So, what are you trying to do to help him, then?"

"Well, I've finally gotten Marissa's dad to take over the case, so I can have a look at all the files. Unfortunately, the evidence is pretty damning."

She scoots up to the edge of her seat cushion. "Well, do you have another plan? Isn't there something else you can do, some other avenue you can take?"

I clear my throat. "Actually, I think there might be. But it's dangerous. Probably very dangerous."

She narrows her eyes. "What is it?"

I stop and think before I continue. This is the only part that could ever really pose a threat to her, although just *knowing* about it shouldn't be dangerous. But still . . .

"I have the books he took."

Her brows shoot up and her eyes get round. "Are you kidding me? You have the books that were so important, so dangerous that someone blew up your father's boat to keep him quiet?"

Even though we are alone, I'm still paranoid. I fight the urge to look over my shoulder. "Yes," I say quietly. "I made him give them to me before he got arrested. I promised him I'd keep them hidden. And safe. Even though they're what got him in trouble in the first place, they're also what's keeping him alive. As long as they know they're out there, we're safe."

"And you think you can use them to . . . what?"

"I wasn't really going to tell you what you were looking at, but I was going to have you look over the books. I've studied them for countless hours over the last few months and I think there is some evidence there that could put some of the higher-ups away for life. If what I suspect is true, these books would prove tax evasion. That, coupled with several other crimes my father knows them to be guilty of, not the least of which is the murder of my brother and mother, could go toward proving racketeering and they could be prosecuted under the RICO Act."

She's perfectly quiet for so long that I wonder if she even understood what I said.

But when she finally says something, I know which part struck her the hardest.

It's the part that makes me look like the bastard most people have always thought me to be.

THIRTY-ONE

Olivia

It's the most bizarre and surreal thing to be looking at the guy I've known as Cash and suddenly see Nash appear. The mussed hair is still all Cash. The casual clothes are still all Cash. Some of the mannerisms are still all Cash. But the speech, the sudden switch into intelligent, successful, soon-to-be attorney mode, is all Nash. And it's staggering.

But not nearly as staggering as his inadvertent admission.

I speak quietly, trying to remain calm. "So what you're saying is that you were going to involve me in something that could potentially get me killed without even telling me? Without giving me so much as a heads-up?" I rise to my feet. I can't help it. Anger is pulsing through me like spray from a fire hose, and I can't remain sitting. If I do, I might explode. "Without giving me a choice?"

At least Cash has the decency to look embarrassed. Ashamed. Contrite. "I'm sure that's what it looks like, but I promise you, I would never put you in danger. I just wanted you to do the numbers, look at the tax code. Give me your opinion. I was going to tell you they were for another business I was considering buying. I knew I could trust you not to say anything if I was right and there were serious violations. If I'd taken it to a CPA, they might've felt compelled to try to get the name of the business and turn them in. Something crazy like that."

Even though that makes it sound a lot less horrific, I'm still having trouble thinking past my anger. Deep down, though, I know it has more to do with being lied to than anything else. Strangely, the rest all sounds like stuff I could deal with, albeit with some liquor, a sedative, and some time to think, but still, I could manage.

But this, this lying . . . I've always hated liars and being lied to more than anything else. To me, it's always been the only truly unforgivable sin.

Can Cash be the first exception? Or has this forever wounded whatever is between us?

"Olivia, please understand that I would never, *never*—"

I put up my hand to stop him. "Stop. Please don't say anything else. I think I've heard enough for one day. Maybe for the rest of my life. I won't know until I've had some time to think."

He looks defeated. Not really worried, like he's afraid I might tell someone, just defeated. Like he took the chance and it backfired. I smother the little pang of guilt for trampling his attempts at coming clean. I can't afford to feel tenderness toward him right now. I need to be practical and rational. Cool. Emotionless.

I pretend to look through my purse. I can't meet his eyes. I'll crumble. I know I will. "Thanks for getting my car fixed and bringing it by. I'll pay you back." I start edging toward the door. Running will only make me look like a coward, even though that's what I'd really *like* to do—run. Far and fast.

Cash says nothing. I don't look up until I'm facing the door and he's to my left. I pause, thinking I should probably say something else but not having the first idea what that is.

I open the door and walk out. I don't look back, but I can feel Cash's eyes follow me until I disappear around the corner.

I've never been the type to skip school a lot. A class or even a day here and there maybe, but nothing substantial. Until now.

Tuesday morning doesn't bring the peace I thought it would. In fact, between getting very little sleep—again—and the magnitude of my troubling thoughts, I feel almost physically ill. My stomach turns over when I see the flowers that Nash left me.

"Cash," I say out loud, correcting myself for the hundredth time.

As I did most of yesterday and far into the night, I relive the humiliation of what happened with Cash when I thought he was Nash. The things I said to him, the way I acted, the things we did. Or nearly did. The way I tortured myself over who had crept into my bedroom that night.

I rock between anger and mortification then back to anger.

How could he do this to me? How could he do this to everyone?

I go to the kitchen to make coffee. As I pass my phone, I see the screen light up. I had put it on vibrate and left it out here last night because I didn't want to be tempted to answer it. The name displayed is "Cash."

I wonder if he'll ever use Nash's phone again when he calls me?

Bitterness courses through me. It's so thick I can almost taste it. Ignoring the call just like I have the half dozen others from him, I continue on to the kitchen.

As I sip my coffee in the living room, I try to think of other things, but they all lead back to the most important issue in my life. Cash.

How did he become such a central theme? When did I get so deeply involved? How had it happened without my knowledge?

The answer? It didn't. I knew I would fall for him. I lied to myself just enough to soften the blow at the time, but I knew it would end like this. It's the story of my life.

Another swell of anger. And bitterness.

Then longing. And loneliness.

The anger again. At Cash for letting me get so close. For drawing me in, like a spider into his web.

His web of lies!

At least there are no tears. I'm thankful for that. Tears are exhausting. Anger is like rocket fuel. Maybe I don't cry because the ball is in my court. Because I know all I have to do is pick up the phone, return one of the many messages he's left me, and I can be with him again. At least for a little while.

In a different web of lies. In a relationship with no future.

THIRTY-TWO

Cash

I hit the red "end" button on the phone. The word itself mocks me. Have I really destroyed any chance to be with Olivia? Do I really care if I have?

The answers are *I don't know* and *Yes*. In that order.

I can only hope coming clean with her was the right decision. I would've thought someone like Olivia would appreciate the gesture, the significance of what I did in the end. But maybe I was wrong. I've never really had feelings for a girl like her. Hell, I've never really had feelings for any girl, period. Not like this, anyway.

I resist the urge to throw my phone across the room. The next step is hers. It's her choice. I'm just going to have to accept that and go along with her decision. Because I won't beg. I won't ever beg a female for anything.

I just won't.

THIRTY-THREE

Olivia

Tuesday melts into Wednesday. Anger and bitterness become depression and devastation. In a way, Cash really was the perfect guy. I'd wanted him to be more like Nash when, in reality, he *was* Nash. He'd turned his life around and made something of himself for his brother, for his father. For his family. He's the perfect blend of bad boy and successful, driven adult. He's everything I ever wanted and everything I ever needed. All wrapped up in one gorgeous, sexy package. Which is all wrapped up in lies and deceit and danger.

If that's not a kick in the ass, I don't know what is.

THIRTY-FOUR

Cash

I guess they're right when they say, "Never say never." I said I would never beg. That's laughable. It's only Wednesday and I've already lost count of how many times I've called Olivia. I should be embarrassed.

But I'm not.

I'm desperate. More and more every day. I'm desperate not to lose her. But I don't know what to do next. I hate to go to her house and force her to talk to me. But I will. At this point, I can't think of anything I wouldn't do for her. To see her. To talk to her. To touch her and taste her again.

Oh damn, this ain't good!

THIRTY-FIVE

Olivia

Wednesday becomes Thursday. My phone is lighting up with more frequency. I keep it close so I can see if it's Dad calling. It never is. Every time I call to check on him, he assures me he's doing well and promises he'll call if he needs anything. But he never does.

Maybe I should just go home for a while. Take a break from school. From life. From heartache. From Cash.

I have only a few more days until Marissa comes home, anyway. And then what will happen? Will "Nash" still be a part of her life? Will he still visit? And hold her and kiss her? Does he tell her he loves her? Did he ever plan a future with her? Will he?

Those thoughts always send me into a tailspin. On the one hand, I knew "Nash" was probably sleeping with her. I mean, they were dating. Of course they were having sex. But I thought Cash was unattached. I thought he was into me. All about me. At least for the time being. As much as a guy like that ever is "into" one specific girl. But it was all a lie.

It was all a lie.

Wasn't it?

THIRTY-SIX

Cash

I take the familiar turns that lead to the prison. I'm at my wits' end. The only thing I can do, short of showing up at Olivia's and doing some serious groveling, is to go talk to Dad. It became apparent to me a couple days ago that I don't know what the hell I'm doing. I'm hoping he'll have some good advice, some good suggestions. I need all the help I can get. And there's only one person, other than Olivia, on the entire planet who knows what's going on.

I committed the visiting hours schedule to memory years ago. I've come to visit Dad both as Cash and as Nash. I never tried to hide my family's past from the upper crust of Atlanta society. I just tried to be involved in it in a completely different way as Nash.

As Nash, I was always approaching it from a legal standpoint, like it was my duty to try to help my father by learning and doing what I could. Legally.

As Cash, I never really did anything. I took the only thing he left me—Dual, something that was bought with questionable money from questionable people—and I turned it into a successful, respectable establishment. Something a kid without a high school diploma could run. Something people would expect a person like me to be involved with. I played Cash to the bone.

But somewhere along the way, I became something else. Something different. Some kind of hybrid. I'm not satisfied being the loser Cash anymore. At least not *only* the loser Cash. I *like* being respect*able* and respect*ed*. I like being looked at like I'm worth something and like my opinion matters. I like other people knowing I'm smart without my having to try to convince them. And then fail. I like being the winner that my brother was.

Only I'm not my brother. I'm a winner all on my own. Yes, his death gave me another chance at life, but I accomplished all these things on my own.

And I'm the only person who will ever know. Except for my father.

And Olivia.

The guards buzz me through the gate and I check in, filling in the blanks and signing my name, identifying the name and number of the prisoner I'm here to see. After I finish, they lead me to the familiar room with one long table cut in half by a wall of glass. It's divided periodically by partitions that create tiny cubicles. They're designed to give the illusion of privacy. But in here, there's no privacy. I have no doubt that everything I say into the nondescript black telephone is taped and stored somewhere. Luckily, my father is innocent. And anything else we talk about, we can do vaguely enough so that no one else would suspect what we're discussing.

Like today, when the guards usher him in and he greets me.

He smiles. "So who's visiting me today? Cash or Nash? I can't tell by the clothes."

I look down at my hastily assembled outfit. I guess, for me at least, it is pretty middle-of-the-road. Black jeans and a striped rugby shirt. It's something that either Cash or Nash might wear. That or neither of them would wear it. I'm not sure which. I can't even remember buying the shirt.

"Does it matter?" I ask dryly.

He smiles again. His eyes search my face, like they do every time I come to visit. Like he's looking for signs of change and age. Or distress. When his smile fades, I know that today he's found some.

He sits up a little straighter, his eyes becoming sharp. Aware. Vigilant. "What's wrong? What's happened?"

"I met a girl."

A frown flickers across his face—the face that most people say looks so much like an older version of my own—but then it smoothes and his lips curve into a very pleased grin. "Well, it's about time. I'll be damned." He sits back and slaps his hand on the table. He's genuinely happy for me. Well, at least until I tell him the rest. That might change his tune.

"I told her, Dad," I say, deadpan.

He looks a little confused for a second before he realizes what all is encompassed in that blanket statement. "How long have you known this girl?"

I start shaking my head. I know where he's going. Always suspicious. "Dad, it doesn't matter. I needed to tell her. I care about her. And I trust her. Besides, I thought maybe she could help."

"Bringing her into all this, that doesn't sound like you care for her at all."

"I had it worked out to keep her safe. I wouldn't put her in danger."

"*You* put her in danger. You're my son. You're in this whether you like it or not. And I'm sorry for that. Sorrier than you'll ever know, but what's done is done. For the rest of *my* life, you'll have to be careful of who you let in. Maybe one day . . . when I'm gone . . ."

"I'm not waiting around, Dad. I'm not gonna let you die in here and I'm not gonna put my life on hold because of some mistakes that were made years ago. We've been punished enough. It's time for us to get on with life. I think I've found a way to—"

"Get yourself killed. That's what you've done. Stop messing in stuff you've got no business messing in, Cash. I gave you those . . . items as insurance. Nothing more."

"Well, I'm sorry, Dad, but I'm tired of letting other people ruin my life. I can't live this way. You're all I've got left. I can't just stand by and do nothing."

"Son, we've talked about this. I appreciate what you're trying to do, but it's just not the smartest—"

"Dad, can't you just trust me? For once, can't you just trust that I'm capable of taking care of things, of making good decisions? Of executing a well-thought-out plan?"

His expression softens. "It's not that I don't trust you. It's that you're all I've got left, too. And I've brought so much misery to your life. I want you to go and live a happy, normal life. A life like you would've had if I'd died in that fire, too."

"Dad, I could never be happy letting you languish in here."

He grins. "Languish?"

I smile. "Law school improved my vocabulary."

He starts to say something, then changes his mind.

"What?" I ask.

"I was just gonna say that I was proud of you *before* you went to law school. Ever since you were young, you were always happy just being you. You were gonna do what you wanted to do, the rest of the world be damned. I was always proud of that tough streak. I've always admired that kind of confidence and self-assurance."

I feel emotion squeeze around my throat like a fist. I guess you never get too old to crave your father's approval. Or at least I haven't yet.

"Cash, please don't let that tough streak make your decisions for you. There's a time to give up, to let things go. If you care about this girl, go find her and make her happy. Keep her safe. Give her a life away from all this. Start fresh. If you love her even half as much as I loved your mother, you'll have a good life. And that's all I want for you."

"Whoa. I didn't say I loved her."

Dad smiles at me. "You didn't have to."

THIRTY-SEVEN

Olivia

Friday morning I make myself get a shower. I find it more than a little disgusting and pathetic that I haven't taken one all week.

But today, I'm done being pathetic. I've wallowed long enough. I've got to do something. So I'm going home for the weekend. I'll call Tad on the way and see if I can pick up at least one shift. After that, I'll figure out what to do for the rest of . . . well, *ever* when I get back.

Just the thought of having to come back and deal with Cash and then Marissa and school and . . . life is so overwhelming. I push it out of my head in favor of a weekend spent in the familiar. In the comforting. In the safe.

Safe. I never thought I'd have such a literal application for that word in my life.

I pack a bag of essentials and head out, locking up behind myself. With Marissa gone and Cash/Nash being out of the picture, I feel completely disconnected from the city. From my life. To my home. It doesn't feel like home right now. It feels like a prison of lies and heartache. The only place that feels like home is the one I'm traveling toward.

I call Dad and Ginger on the way. Ginger is kind enough to offer me one of her shifts, which I gladly accept. It'll be tonight's shift, which is probably a good thing. I can stay busy right off the bat. Tomorrow, I'll go out and look for more lambs, even though there's no real reason. But it'll be good to get outside, to do something that doesn't require me to think. Or hurt. Or want.

"Hey, punk," Dad says by way of greeting when I walk in. I have the sudden and inexplicable urge to go throw my arms around his neck and cry on his shoulder like I did when I was a kid. Rather than doing that, however, and scaring the crap out of him, I set my bag down and go kiss him on the cheek and ask how he's been.

I spend the day watching a *CSI* rerun marathon on television and chatting about this and that. It doesn't completely get Cash off my brain, but it helps. I knew it would.

I shower and dress for my shift, happily slipping into the emotional comfort of the black shorts and tee as much as I slip into the physical comfort of them. I get Dad settled before I go, and then I drive myself to Tad's.

Everyone is awesome. Of course. Glad to have me back. I feel tears threaten more than once when regulars ask me to come back, assuring me that they'll never be as good to me at my new job as they are at Tad's. In a way, I believe them. But in a way, I also know that's not true. Cash is at my new job.

Cash.

Ginger shows up, not to work, but to provide much-needed support from the other side of the bar. She sips her drink and waits patiently for things to slow down before she asks any questions.

"So, let me guess. 'Bad boy' turned out to be 'worst boy'?"

I laugh. Yes, it's a little bitter. "Um, I guess you could say that."

"I was afraid of that."

I stop stocking beer bottles into the cooler and stare at her, mouth agape. "You were? Well, you could've said something, you know."

"I took one look at him and knew he was trouble. He's not just hot. He's smart. That's not a good combination for your heart, Liv. At least the others have been pretty useless and stupid. But this one? Yeah, I knew if he got his hooks into you there'd be trouble."

I'd like to slap her. Hard. "Thanks for the heads-up, Ginger," I say, trying to sound teasing but knowing my anger is showing.

"Would you have listened to me if I'd tried? No. You never do. You knew you should've stayed away from him. But you didn't. Do you really think I could've said anything that would've changed your mind?"

I don't want to admit it, but she's probably right. Cash had me breathless from day one. So did Nash. Because they were the same guy, only in different clothes and with different jobs. I think, deep down, my body knew. I responded to each of them the same way, sexually. They both set me on fire. And that's not too likely to happen with two such supposedly different personalities. Why didn't I see it? How could I be so blind?

I'm emptying the last of the bottles from the box, arranging them neatly in the cooler, when I see someone slide onto the stool beside Ginger. I look up and stop, my arm halfway into the cooler.

It's Cash.

He doesn't smile. He doesn't say anything. He just looks at me. I wonder if that's his heart I see in this eyes. Or if it's just my imagination. Either way, I don't trust it. I don't trust *him*.

I say nothing. I finish what I'm doing, take the box into the back, then come back out and pour him a Jack neat. I slide him the glass, he slides me a twenty, and I pay for the drink and stick the change in the tip jar. I throw a smug look at him, daring him to make a comment. But he's smart. He doesn't say a word, just nods and tosses back his whiskey.

I don't need to ask what he's doing here. I only listened to one of his dozen or so messages, and it was him asking to talk to me. I saved the rest. I figured I'd listen to them eventually. Just not yet.

A guy who is widely known to adore Ginger sits on her other side and starts chatting her up, leaving me to tend to the few other customers at the bar. And Cash.

I keep myself busy with odd jobs, but it doesn't really help.

Every nerve, every cell, every sense of my entire being is focused sharply on Cash.

Cash.

By the time the night is over, I'm on edge. He still hasn't said a word. Neither have I. But the tension is palpable. And it's killing me.

When Tad gives last call, Cash looks at me long and hard, then slides off his stool and walks out. I feel aggravated and bereft and sad and frustrated and hurt. But mostly I feel like chasing him. Like asking him to stay.

But I don't.

I can't.

I won't.

As we are required to do, the bartenders stay as Tad counts the till. But my mind is wandering. To Cash. Always to Cash.

Taking my phone out of my pocket, I check for messages. There are no new ones, which both puzzles and disappoints me, so I randomly select one of the saved messages from him and listen to it. When his voice comes on, there is a quick, sharp stab of pain in my chest.

"Look, Olivia, I care about you. Can't you see that? Can't you feel it? I might not have always done the right thing, but try to see it from my perspective. Do you know how hard it was for me to tell you all this? Knowing that you might leave and never come back? I was just hoping that you wouldn't do that. Leave. But you did. And I know I should let you go. But I can't. I just can't."

I hear him sigh into the phone and then it clicks off.

A lump of emotion constricts my throat.

What am I supposed to do? He's a liar. A liar!

Some small voice pipes up to tell me that he had a better-than-average reason to lie and that he did finally come clean, trusting me with things that could literally threaten his life.

Does that matter?

The small voice answers that it does. It matters very much.

I choose another message to listen to.

"Okay, if this is how you're gonna play it, fine! I've done all I can do. I've tried to help you, to show you I care about you, but obviously that's not enough. Maybe you're right. Maybe you're right to go. I don't even know anymore."

I listen to another and another and another. It's plain that Cash was going through all manner of reactions to *my* reaction. For some reason, they make my heart squeeze. The one thing that's apparent in all of them is that he's searching desperately for some way to fix things. And that I'm the one making him desperate. I know what that feels like. I know what it's like to care about someone so much they make you desperate.

But it doesn't matter. It *shouldn't* matter.

But it does *matter.*

I just get more irritated.

When Tad's finished and he's ready to lock up, we all leave together. As I approach my car, I see Cash sitting on his motorcycle, right beside the driver's side. I walk past him, unlock my door, get inside, and start the engine. I consider rolling down my window to talk to him, but I decide against it.

As I pull out of the lot and turn toward home, I see a single light, the headlight of Cash's motorcycle, pull out behind me.

Is he following me home? What's he gonna do, cause a scene in front of my father? My father with the broken leg?

My irritation rises. But so does that swelling sensation in my chest, like my heart might burst from inside my ribs. Like *Alien*.

Cash's messages run through my mind—his words, the sound of his voice, the things he doesn't say, as well as the things that come across so clear. I look in my rearview mirror again, at the bike's front light. Following me. Steadily, persistently following me. Like his focus is as bright and singular as the headlight.

As I pass a familiar pull-off that's hidden in the trees along the road, I swerve into it, coming to a crunchy stop in the gravel. Impulsively, angrily, I throw the gearshift into park, shut off the lights, and get out, slamming the door behind me. Within seconds, Cash is pulling to a stop behind me and cutting his engine, too.

I stomp over to where he's taking off his helmet and getting off the bike. "What the hell do you want from me?" I scream, anger suddenly finding its way back to the forefront. I lash out, putting my palms in the center of his broad chest and pushing with all my might. He barely moves. "What are you trying to do to me?"

When I feel tears threaten, I turn and walk quickly back to my car. As I'm rounding the hood, I feel fingers like steel bands wrap around my upper arms and bring me to a stop. Cash whirls me to face him. In the silvery light of the full moon, I can see the livid set to his features, the flash of temper in his eyes.

"Stop! Just stop!" he spits.

"Why? What else needs to be said? I think you've told me enough lies for a lifetime."

"No more lies," he says angrily. "I don't even *want* to talk to you anymore. I just want to hear you tell me that you don't feel anything for me. That you want me to leave you alone and never come back. Then I'll go. If that's what you really want, I'll go."

I know this is my opportunity. In my gut, I believe that he'll do exactly what he says—he'll be gone from my life forever if I tell him to go.

I open my mouth to speak, but no words come out. I hear him gasp, as if he's waiting for me to banish him from my life.

Rage drains from his face. It's replaced by something close to a silent plea. Then he whispers.

"Don't. Please don't say it."

I search his eyes. For what, I don't know. "Why?"

"Because I don't want you to. I need you to come back to me. Not to help me. Or to help my father. I'm done with that. I don't want your help. It all boils down to you. I just want you."

My heart is beating wildly inside my chest. I hear nothing, feel nothing, see nothing but Cash. And even so, I barely hear him whisper again, "I just want you."

Before I can give it another second's thought, before I can overthink it and torture myself with what I *should* do rather than what I *want* to do, I answer him quietly. "Okay."

I see several emotions flicker across his face, but then I see nothing. I'm in his arms.

His lips crash down on mine and the world disappears. My fingers are in his hair, holding him to me. His hands are roaming my back and hips.

And then he's lifting me onto the hood of the car. Kissing my neck, untucking my shirt, touching my breasts.

I wrap my legs around his slim hips and pull him into the V of my thighs. He grinds against the place I need him most.

His fingers loosen the button and zipper to my shorts. I'm only vaguely aware of being thankful we are so hidden from the road.

With his palm, he pushes me back onto the hood and pulls my shorts and panties down over my feet. He tosses them onto the car beside me and lifts my bent legs onto his shoulders, burying his face between them.

I can't hold in the moans of pleasure his tongue elicits. I feel it making hot circles over my clitoris. I feel it lick down and slide inside me, pushing in as deep as it will go. I feel him rub his face against me. And then I feel the world explode around him, showering him with the fireworks of my orgasm.

He moves and then I hear his zipper. He enters me and my spasms continue. He grabs my hips and pulls me tighter against him, my back still pressed to the warm metal of my car.

I look up through half-lidded eyes and I see him watching me, so serious, so sensual. He moves his hand between us and I jump when his thumb grazes my sensitive clitoris. But he's gentle and, soon enough, I feel the tension building again. I close my eyes and just feel.

The waves of one orgasm run seamlessly into the next. As my body squeezes Cash, I feel him pulse within me. He spreads through me as he fills me up, as he comes deep inside me.

I open my eyes again and see his back arched and his head thrown back. It's so hot to watch him come, I feel my body reacting, milking him, demanding everything he has to give. I want it all. I want everything he has to offer. I want it pouring out inside me.

With his body still shooting hot liquid into mine, Cash opens his eyes and reaches for my hands, pulling me up and into his arms. We are as joined as two people can be. And not just physically.

He showers my face with kisses and runs his hands all over my back. He doesn't need to use words. I know what he's saying. I perceive it. I feel it. And I feel the same way.

THIRTY-EIGHT

Cash

I open my eyes to bright streaks of light peeking under the edges of the curtains in Olivia's room. I shouldn't have stayed as long as I did, but I wanted to hold her while she slept. I wanted her to know I wasn't going anywhere. That she's safe with me. In my arms.

Unfortunately, I fell asleep, too. Great sex for the third time in a short period of time does that to me.

I smile and I look down at Olivia where she's curled up against me, her beautiful face relaxed in sleep.

I don't want to put names to the things I feel for her. I just want her to know I'm not going anywhere. And that I want to take care of her. To make her happy. I hope that's enough. It has to be.

She wiggles against me and I feel my body react. I know if

I don't get out of bed, I'll end up waking her. And while that sounds like the best possible start to my day, I know she'll be sore if I don't give her a break. Besides, her father will be up soon and I need to get to my own room.

Easing out from under her, I slip on my jeans and grab the rest of my clothes, tiptoeing to the door. I crack it and listen. It sounds like her dad is already stirring.

Silently, I sneak to the bathroom and take a quick shower. When I'm done, I head downstairs, letting Olivia sleep as long as she can.

Darrin, Olivia's father, is sitting at the kitchen table. The way he's watching me, I can't help but think he was waiting for me.

I nod. "Good morning, sir."

He nods in return. "So, you're the one," he says enigmatically.

I look into his eyes, a more brown and less bright version of Olivia's, and I know what he's getting at, what he wants to know. Straightening to my full height, I link my hands behind my back and nod again. "Yes, sir. I am."

His eyes travel me from head to toe, measuring me up like he might measure a new ram for his flock, before they come to rest on mine. They speak volumes as they look, unwaveringly, at me. Into me.

"And you know what she means to me, what I would do for her. And to anyone who hurt her."

I suppress the grin that twitches at the corners of my mouth. He *sounds* about Olivia like I *feel* about Olivia. "Yes, sir."

After several more long, tense seconds, he finally nods. "All right, then let's get that girl some breakfast."

From that point on, I can't seem to wipe the smile from my face.

Sometime later, when Darrin speaks to Olivia, I turn to see her standing at the kitchen door. She looks adorably tousled. It makes me want to pick her up and carry her back to bed.

I find myself holding my breath when she looks at me. I'm a little uneasy. I don't know if the bright light of day has brought about some new revelation that will work against me.

When she smiles shyly at me, I exhale. And when her cheeks turn pink, I chuckle. I don't know why that makes me so happy. But it does.

"Good morning," I say, laying my spatula in the big spoon that sits to the right of the stove. I know her father knows how I feel about her, but even if I didn't, I couldn't stop myself from going to her.

I stop in front of Olivia and cup her face in my hands, kissing her sweetly on the mouth. She looks up at me with her liquid eyes and something in me melts away. I think to myself that I hope it wasn't something important. Something that I needed.

It makes me just a little uncomfortable, feeling the things I feel for her, so I give her a smile and head back to the stove, hoping she won't see my uncertainty.

The rest of the morning goes smoothly. Right up until she announces that we're heading back to the city after lunch. My head jerks up and our eyes meet. There's no warning in them, but there's a purpose. There's no mistaking that.

"Why so soon, Liv?" Darrin asks.

"I've got some things to take care of, Dad." I see her eyes flicker up to mine where I'm sitting across the table from her. "Marissa will be back soon and I've got some things to figure out."

There it is.

We've got some things to figure out. Obviously.

THIRTY-NINE

Olivia

The ride back to the city is as different from the ride away as it's possible to get. The only thing that would make it more dramatic is if my hair were on fire or I were a man.

I glance back periodically to see Cash on his bike, following along behind me. He's wearing his helmet, so I can't even see his eyes, but I imagine that he smiles at me each time I look back. I can almost feel it. A couple of times, he even nods, like he can tell I'm looking at him. I wonder if he can see my eyes shift to him in the rearview mirror . . .

When I pull into one of the spots designated for Marissa's townhouse, Cash pulls in beside me, killing his engine and taking off his helmet. I try to hide the smile I feel that he's coming in without me having to ask. It's like some unspoken agreement has been reached between us. I'm his and he's mine. At least for now. And I refuse to think any further than that.

He carries my bag in and takes it into my room. Rather than just dropping it, he sets it on the bed and sits down beside it. Before I can ask what he's doing, he clears his throat.

"Why don't you pack a bigger bag and come stay with me?"

My stomach flutters at the thought of going to sleep in Cash's arms every night and waking up in them every morning. Of going to sleep with his taste on my tongue and waking up with his tongue in my mouth. That's what it would be like. At least for a while. For a few days.

It sounds like heaven.

But then, as it so often does at the most inopportune times, reality intrudes. And I think of Marissa.

"Look, Cash, I understand why you've done what you've done and how important it is, but I can't pretend now that you aren't Nash. That when Nash is sleeping with Marissa, it's not you. Because it is. And it always has been."

Cash reaches for my hands and pulls me into the space between his spread legs. When he looks up at me, his dark eyes are sparkling. My breath hitches in my chest.

"I broke up with Marissa on Wednesday."

I ignore the fact that my heart feels like a balloon that someone filled up and then let go before tying it off, like it's soaring around the room at the speed of light. "You did?"

"I did."

I'm almost afraid to ask. But I do. "Why?"

"Because she's not the one I want to be with."

"But you work with her father."

"I already talked to him, too."

"You did?"

He laughs. "Yes. I'm done with all that . . . stuff. I can't really tell people that Nash is dead, but I don't have to continue on the same path. I'm letting Dad's case go. Moving on. I'll finish my internship and then decide what to do, whether I want to practice, where and how. I'm not letting the past rule my future anymore."

While I appreciate what he's saying, something bothers me. "But he's your only family. And he's in prison. If you can get him out, if there's any chance at all, don't you think you should still try?"

He looks down at our joined hands. He rubs his thumbs over my knuckles. "I haven't felt like I've had a real home in years." Cash pauses and looks up, his eyes meeting mine. They are warm. They are sweet. They are sincere. "Until I met you. *You* feel like home. And that's more important than anything else. You're my home now. You're what matters."

I want to kiss him. And hold him. And tell him I love him.

Do I love him?

The answer comes quickly.

Yes. I do.

But he hasn't said those words to me. So I don't say them to him. But I feel them.

"But if there's something you can do to help him, I want you to try. Don't abandon him because of me. I'll help you however I can. I'm not afraid." It's just as I speak the words that I realize I'm not. I'm not afraid. And it's because of Cash. And what I see in his eyes. "I know you won't put me in danger. Not on purpose." I tug one of my hands loose and trace his strong, square jaw with my fingertips. "I trust you, Cash. I trust you."

He grabs my wrist and presses his lips to the inside, then pulls gently until I'm bent at the waist and my face is close to his.

"Come home with me. Please." I can feel his warm breath on my lips, they're so close. I lean forward to close the small gap, but he leans away. "Please," he repeats softly.

I would never tell him, but he could ask me anything right now and I'd agree to it. Anything at all.

"Okay." As soon as the words leave my lips, his mouth is on mine.

His hands are hungry and urgent as he grabs me around the waist and turns to lay me on the bed. We undress each other as though we've never made love, as though this is the first time and we can't wait one more second to feel skin on skin.

When he enters me, my whole world collapses. It melts and covers us as he moves within me, like a perfect crystalline cocoon. And when we are both satisfied and breathing heavily, Cash lays his forehead against mine and whispers, "Home."

I think to myself that this is the very moment when I'm lost. Lost to Cash. Forever.

FORTY

Cash

As I straighten up my condo, I can't help but recognize that I've probably never felt more positive about life. Even before the "accident" I didn't feel so good about the future. So optimistic. So . . . enthused.

And the difference?

Olivia.

I smile and shake my head as I think of her. She wanted to take a shower and clean up before she packed and headed over here. She suggested I go ahead. I'm not really surprised, I don't guess. I know how girls are, what with their need for grooming time and personal space. So I kissed her and left. The strange thing is, I had to make myself leave rather than join her in the shower. I don't know what it is about her, but I can't seem to get enough. Even when I've had enough, I want more.

When my phone rings, I pull it out and check the screen. It says simply, "Olivia." I smile wider.

"You're supposed to be over here by now. What's taking you so long?"

There's a pause before she speaks. When she does, I hear her shy voice. "Um, I don't know what kind of, um, *plans* you have for us tonight. Should I bring work clothes for tonight and tomorrow night? Or . . . ?"

"You haven't met him yet, but I have a guy that helps manage the bar. His name is Gavin and I already had him rework the schedule to cover your shifts this weekend. Why don't you just take the time off and spend it with me?"

She laughs a little and when she answers, I can hear the smile in her voice. "I'd love to spend the weekend with you doing . . . whatever, but I really can't afford to miss much more time."

I'm smart enough and an astute enough observer of women to know offering her money would be a huge mistake. So, to keep the peace, I do what I need to. "Well, then just plan to work tomorrow night. Will that be enough, since you worked last night at Tad's?"

"Yeah, I think that'll be fine."

"All right then. Get your ass over here."

"On my way," she chirps, and then the line goes dead.

I wonder if I'll ever stop smiling and, if I can't, what kind of excuse I'll have to make up to explain it. Or if I'll even bother. Because at the moment, I just don't give a shit. I'm happy. She's happy. That's all that matters.

FORTY-ONE

Olivia

Cash didn't say where to park, so I stick with the lot out front, just to be safe. I'll probably need to move it later, so as not to announce to everyone I'm getting preferential treatment because I'm screwing the boss.

I can't help but grin. That sounds so trashy, but I just don't care. I refuse to let anything or anyone ruin this happy time of my life. Happy times come by so infrequently, I'm determined to enjoy them as much as I can, *while* I can.

Retrieving my bag and purse from the backseat, I lock the doors and head around the side entrance to the apartment. Butterflies are alive and well in my stomach, which is kind of ridiculous considering that I've had sex with Cash well over a dozen times. But still . . .

The garage door is open as I approach. So is the interior

door. And Cash is standing just inside it, smiling. He stops me from entering and takes my bag and purse from me, setting them on the floor behind him. Then, with a wicked grin, he sweeps me up into his arms and carries me inside, kicking the door shut with his heel.

"I'm supposed to carry you over the threshold, right?"

I laugh. "If that's what you're doing, I must've slept through something important," I say dryly.

He quirks one eyebrow and shoots me a cocky grin. "Oh trust me, I won't let you sleep through any of the good stuff."

I wrap my arms more tightly around his neck and he bends his head to kiss me. When his lips meet mine, there is fire, just like always. But there's something else, too. Something deeper, sweeter. More meaningful. It makes my heart sing like his kiss makes my toes curl.

He carries me into the bedroom and lays me down on the bed. He starts to lie down beside me, but I stop him. This time is different. It *feels* different. And I want to start things off with a bang. Pun intended.

I come up onto my knees and move to the edge of the bed. Smiling up into his eyes, I don't say a word. I just set about untucking his shirt. Just like I was doing the first time we met. It takes only a few seconds for understanding to dawn on him. And I know the instant it does. His lips twitch and his brow rises, much like that first night, and he spreads his arms out, away from his body, also much like he did that first night.

I giggle as I stand up on the bed to peel his shirt off him and toss it aside. I can't think of a more perfect way to start this new leg of our relationship. It's almost like we've come full circle and we're getting another chance. And if that's the case, I plan to make the most of it.

Dropping back onto my knees, I place my mouth over one flat nipple, flicking it with my tongue until it forms a tight bud, then sucking it into my mouth. I hear him gasp.

"Even then, I knew you'd be a handful."

I look up at him as I drag my lips down his stomach. My fingers are already working his zipper loose.

"Baby, you have no idea."

I know by his smile that he's happy. And that's all that matters.

Nearly an hour later, Cash is resting on top of me, his weight braced on his forearms. We've been lying like this for several minutes, just enjoying the feel of him softening inside me, the feel of his skin against mine, the feel of the world so quiet around us.

When Cash lifts his head and looks down into my eyes, there's a wealth of emotion in the dazzling depths, so much so that it brings tears to my eyes. I think of what he told me earlier and I smile up at him. Cupping his handsome face, I whisper against his lips, "Welcome home."

When he kisses me, I know we're both where we belong.

Duffy

The lock was too easy to pick. Duffy thinks it's funny that rich people think they're safe, think they're protected against any intruders as long as they've got a security system. He actually laughs out loud before he shushes himself.

If they only knew . . .

Making his way through the darkened rooms, Duffy finds what he's looking for—her bedroom.

Duffy will be making a call to the landlord at midnight, complaining of a television being left on too loud. In this townhouse. He'll demand that the tenant be notified and ordered to reduce the noise. She'll come home to take care of it and Duffy will be waiting for her. With his van parked outside.

Duffy is nothing if not patient. He'll see a good plan through to the bitter end. And theirs is a good plan. They only need her long enough to get the books. And then Duffy can get rid of them both. Easy peasy.

Moving to the space behind her bedroom door, Duffy dials the landlord's number to make the false report. When he hangs up, he calls his boss.

"Yeah, I'll bring her tonight. I'll have you the books by sunrise. Then I'll get rid of them both."

Flipping his ancient cell phone shut and stuffing it in his pocket, Duffy settles in to wait.

For Olivia Townsend.

To be continued . . .

A FINAL WORD

A few times in life, I've found myself in a position of such love
and gratitude that saying THANK YOU seems trite, like it's
just not enough. That is the position that I find myself in now
when it comes to you, my readers. You are the sole reason that
my dream of being a writer has come true. I knew that it would
be gratifying and wonderful to finally have a job that I loved
so much, but I had no idea that it would be outweighed and
outshined by the unimaginable pleasure that I get from hearing that you love my work, that it's touched you in some way
or that your life seems a little bit better for having read it. So
it is from the depths of my soul, from the very bottom of my
heart that I say I simply cannot THANK YOU enough. I've
added this note to all my stories with the link to a blog post
that I really hope you'll take a minute to read. It is a true and

sincere expression of my humble appreciation. I love each and every one of you and you'll never know what your many encouraging posts, comments, and emails have meant to me.

http://mleightonbooks.blogspot.com/2011/
06/when-thanks-is-not-enough.html

Keep reading for an excerpt from
the next Bad Boys book

UP TO ME

Available in August 2013 from Berkley Books

ONE

Olivia

Out of the corner of my eye, I see the light flicker at the back of Dual. The door to Cash's office opens and closes as he comes out into the club. He looks up and our eyes lock instantly. His expression is carefully schooled, per my request, but that doesn't mean my toes don't curl inside my work shoes. His eyes are blazing as they look into mine. My stomach does a flip and then he looks away, which is a very good thing. Otherwise, it wouldn't be Cash who blew our cover, it would be me—when I leave my position behind the bar, march right over to him, plant my lips on his, and then drag him back to bed.

Tearing my eyes away from him, I force my mind back to my job.

Dammit.

"I got it," Taryn chirps, reaching in front of me to grab a dirty glass from the bar top.

I smile and nod my thanks, but inside I'm picking her crazy, dreadlocked motives apart. She's been nice to me all night and I'm not sure why. She's never been nice to me. Openly hostile, yes. Spitefully devious, yes. But nice? Oh no. Before tonight, I would've assured anyone who asked that Taryn would rather sharpen her toothbrush into a shiv and shank me than even look at me.

And yet, here she is, smiling my way and bussing my side of the bar.

Hmmm.

I'm not a naturally suspicious person, so . . .

Okay, so I'm a naturally suspicious person, but I have good reason to be. A lifetime of schemers, liars, selfish buttmunchers, and all-around icky people has made me a bit jaded. But I'm coming around.

Anyway, I am extremely curious to know what Taryn's got up her sleeve. And there *is* something up her tattooed sleeve. I'd bet my life on it. Or her life. Either way.

I can almost see the wheels turning behind the blue of her almond-shaped, kohl-lined eyes.

The only thing I can do, however, is watch my back and keep my eyes open. She'll slip up and show her hand eventually. Then I'll know what's going on in that twisted mind of hers. Until then, I'm more than happy to let her kiss my fluffy butt and help as much as she wants.

"So," she begins casually as she makes her way back to me.

"Got plans for tonight after work? I thought maybe we could hit Noir and have a drink, get to know each other a little better."

All right, this is getting ridiculous.

I stare at her, working to keep my jaw from dropping open as I wait for the punch line.

Only there isn't one. She's *serious.*

"You're serious."

She smiles and nods. "Of course I'm serious. Why would I ask if I weren't?"

"Um, because you hate me," I blurt.

Dammit! There goes keeping my eyes peeled and letting her continue on with her ruse.

"I don't hate you. What on earth gave you that idea?"

Oh. My. God. Does she really think I'm that stupid?

I turn to Taryn and fold my arms over my chest. I'm not even supposed to be here. Cash and I just got back from Salt Springs a few hours ago. Gavin had my shift covered since Cash didn't know if I'd be coming back or not. And yet here I am, working to fill in for Marco when I should be naked, wrapped up in Cash's arms. I don't want the patience to play games.

"Look, I'm not sure who you're trying to fool, but if it's me, you might as well give it up. I'm on to you, Taryn."

She opens her pouty ruby lips like she's going to argue, but then she snaps them shut. Her innocently pleasant expression settles into something a little more normal for her and she sighs.

"Okay, I admit I was a little jealous of you when you started here. I don't know if you knew this or not, but Cash and I used to date. Until recently, we were still . . . resolving some things. I thought you might be trying to get in the way of that. But now I know you're not. Besides, I know he's not interested in you. He's got someone else on the hook, so it wouldn't matter, anyway."

That piques my curiosity. "Why do you say that?"

"What? That he's got someone else on the hook? Because I've seen him with a blond girl a couple times and he's been very, very distracted lately. And that's not like him. He's not the one-girl type of guy."

"He's not?"

"Oh, hell no! I knew that going in. Any girl who goes into a relationship with Cash thinking she'll change him or that she'll be the only one is dumber than a box of her long blond hair."

"Blond? Because of the girl you think he's seeing?"

Taryn shrugs. "Her, too, but Cash has a *type*," she says, quirking one pierced brow at me and holding up a pale twist of her hair. "Blond."

I nod and smile, trying my best to seem unaffected. Which I'm not, of course. Far from it. In fact, I'm so affected I feel like I might hurl right in Taryn's pretty face.

"What makes you think he'll never pick one of these . . . blondes and settle down?"

Her laugh is bitter. "Because I know Cash. That boy has wild blood. Guys like that don't change. And girls can't make 'em. It's just the way they are. It's part of why they're so irresistible, too. Don't we all want what we can't have?"

I smile again, but say nothing. After a few seconds, she grabs my towel and swipes at a wet glass ring on the bar. "Anyway, I'm over it. I just wanted you to know I'm burying the hatchet."

"I'm glad," I manage to squeak out past the lump in my throat.

I busy myself with early cleanup duties. Dual is less than an hour from last call. How in the world I'll make it that long is beyond me, but I know the first step is to keep busy. But no amount of busywork can silence the conflicting voices in my head.

You knew he was a bad boy. That's why you tried to stay away from him and not get involved.

I feel dismay curl in the pit of my stomach like a cold, heartless snake. But then the voice of reason—or is it the voice of denial?—speaks up.

After all that has happened over the last few weeks, how can you doubt the way he feels about you? Cash isn't the type to fake it. And what he's said, what you've shared isn't fake. It's real. And it's deep. And Taryn is a psychotic bitch who has no clue what she's talking about. Maybe all that tattoo ink has gone to her brain.

While all of that is true, nothing I tell myself eradicates the feeling of unease that has settled into my bones. Into my heart.

One part of me—the rational, logical, uninvolved, hurt-too-many-times part—pops up to make matters worse.

How many times are you gonna fall for the same lines? The same kind of guy?

But Cash is different. I know it. Deep down. I remind myself that it's completely unfair to judge a book by its cover. No matter how much experience I have with similar covers. Cash's cover might be that of a bad boy, but the book, the *inside*, is so much more.

As I clean the grate under the beer tap, my eyes wander the thinning crowd and dark interior of the club, looking for Cash. Wouldn't you know that when I find him, a busty blond bombshell is throwing her arms around his neck and rubbing her skanky little body all over him. I grit my teeth against the urge to jump over the bar, march right over there, and snatch her bald-headed.

But my anger fades into acute distress when I see Cash smile down into her face. I see his lips move as he speaks to her and my heart springs a leak. It makes me feel somewhat better when he reaches up to unwind her arms from around his neck then takes a step back from her, but it'll take more than that to get Taryn's unwelcome words out of my head.

Dammit.

My mood circles the drain for the next half hour. Even the fairly likable personality Taryn has adopted when she's not being an utter bitch doesn't help. I even start thinking to myself that maybe it would be a good idea to go back to the house for the night.

A bit later, as I wash the sliced-lemons container on my end of the bar, I'm still pondering my options while debating the likelihood that I have undiagnosed bipolar disorder. A shot glass slides across the bar in front of me. I look up to see Taryn at my right, grinning, holding a glass of her own.

"Shhh," she says with a wink. "I won't tell if you won't. It's closing time, anyway." She pulls a ten-dollar bill out of her pocket and throws it down.

At least she's paying.

Normally, I would politely decline, but a shot to calm my nerves and ease my troubled thoughts sounds like a good idea. I wipe my hands on a towel and grab the tiny glass.

Taryn raises hers and smiles at me. "Salut!" she exclaims with a nod.

I nod and raise mine as well, and we both toss back our shot. I don't need to ask what she poured. The vodka burns all the way down.

Making a deep, growly "ah" sound, Taryn grins at me. "Come out with me. You look like you need a night of frivolous fun."

Before I can answer her, Cash's voice interrupts us. "Olivia," he calls from the doorway of his office. "Come see me before you go. There are a few things I need to discuss with you."

"Okay," I reply, my stomach tightening with a mixture of excitement, desire, and dread. He ducks back into his office and closes the door. I turn to Taryn. "Next time?"

"Sure," she responds pleasantly. "I'll just finish up and head out."

She wanders back down to her end of the bar, and it occurs to me that we might actually make it to being friends one day.

Go figure.

I piddle around a little, slowing down enough that Taryn can finish before I go back to "meet" with Cash.

"Tada!" she exclaims, throwing her towel in the sanitizer to soak. "All right, Livvi, I'm outta here. Wish you could come, but duty calls." She tips her head toward Cash's office and rolls her eyes. Grabbing her purse from the shelf under the counter, Taryn circles around to approach me from the other side of the long, black bar. Planting her hands on the shiny surface, she leans forward and gives me an air peck like she's kissing each cheek. "Night, doll."

I'm still struggling with disbelief as I watch her walk through the door and out into the night, dreadlocks swinging. I decide that dramatic personality shifts like that *can't* be healthy.

The instant the front door thumps shut, Cash's office door opens. He emerges, his expression hard and determined. With purpose, he crosses the empty room and locks the double doors behind Taryn.

For a few seconds, all that I've been worrying about for the last couple of hours fades away like the space his long stride eats up so effortlessly. I'm mesmerized just watching him, the way he moves. His long, muscular legs flex with each step. His perfect butt shifts behind the pockets of his jeans. His wide shoulders are square and straight above his trim waist.

And then he turns toward me.

I might never get used to how handsome he is. It might never fail to leave me breathless. His nearly black eyes bore hot holes into mine. They don't break contact as he crosses the room again, this time toward me.

He hops over the bar and lands beside me. Without a word, he bends, throws me over his shoulder, and carries me down the length of the bar and through the cutout on the other end.

My heart is pounding as he takes me through the office and into his apartment on the other side. My body is on fire with desire and anticipation for what's to come, but my mind is still harboring some doubt and insecurity from earlier. I'm debating whether to say something to him and go back home for the night or just ignore every shred of rational thought and stay, when he sets me on my feet.

Immediately, his lips cover mine and all other considerations are gone. He pushes me back against the front door. I feel it click shut behind me.

He takes my hands and brings my arms above my head, pinning my wrists together in the long fingers of one hand. His free hand blazes a fiery trail down my side, his thumb grazing my already-aching nipple, then on to my stomach, where it slips beneath the hem of my tank top.

He flattens his palm over my ribs and moves it around to my back and down into the waistband of my pants. The fit is loose there, so it's easy for him to slide into them, then down into my panties to cup my bare butt.

He pulls me against him, grinding his hips into mine as he sucks on my lower lip. "Do you know how hard it was to let you work tonight? To know that I can't touch you or kiss you or even watch you?" he pants against my open mouth. "All I could think about was what you look like naked and the little noises you make when I stick my tongue inside you."

His words make the lowest part of my belly fill with heat and tighten. He releases my wrists, but rather than push him away, I thread my fingers into his hair and crush my lips to his. I feel him working at the button and zipper of my jeans, and excitement floods me.

"It's only been a few hours and all I can think about is the way you taste, the way you feel wrapped around me. When you're so hot and so ready. So wet," he murmurs against my mouth.

Just as my need rises to fever pitch, a voice interrupts us.

"Nash?" It's Marissa and she's pounding on the interior garage door. Cash drags his lips away from mine and places his finger over my mouth to hush me. "Nash?" She bangs again. "I know you're in there. The garage is open and your car is here."

I hear Cash growl. "Shit! What the hell is she doing back?" he whispers.

My mind races. Although I know Cash and Nash are the same person, the fact that Marissa *doesn't* could pose a problem in instances like this, especially when she doesn't know about Cash and me.

"What should we do? We can't let her find out like this!"

Cash sighs and leans back to run his fingers through his mussed hair. Luckily, his preferred style is kind of spiky and disheveled, so it's not noticeable that my fingers have been in it.

My body aches with want, but my mind is already in gear for reality.

"Well, I guess the only thing to do is pretend like you're closing up. I'll think of something to tell her about Nash."

"Okay," I say, straightening my clothes and hair.

"I could kick myself for opening the garage door so early. I was gonna pull your car in after Taryn left." He sighs again and shakes his head slightly. When he looks back at me, his eyes are smoky and hot. "We're far from finished, though," he promises, leaning in and lightly biting my shoulder. A bolt of electricity shoots through me and lands between my legs. He knows exactly what to do and what to say to tear me up.

Dammit.

ABOUT THE AUTHOR

New York Times and *USA Today* bestselling author **M. Leighton** is a native of Ohio. She relocated to the warmer climates of the South, where she can be near the water all summer and miss the snow all winter. Possessed of an overactive imagination from early in her childhood, Michelle finally found an acceptable outlet for her fantastical visions: literary fiction. Having written more than a dozen novels, Michelle enjoys letting her mind wander to more romantic settings with sexy Southern guys, much like the one she married and the ones you'll find in her latest books. When her thoughts aren't roaming in that direction, she'll be riding wild horses, skiing the slopes of Aspen, or scuba diving with a hot rock star, all without leaving the cozy comfort of her office. Visit her on Facebook, Twitter, Goodreads, and at mleightonbooks .blogspot.com.